INSTA-HEART!

Online and Offline:

A Journey of Love

PRATICHI SANAYE

INDIA · SINGAPORE · MALAYSIA

ISBN 979-8-89277-226-6

Contents

Foreword

"Love is the magnetic force that draws us through screens, immersing us in a maze of emotions where the online and the real collide."

I met Pratichi at the office; she was a digital marketer, and I was a Senior Content Writer. Our collaboration on various projects sparked a deep friendship. I vividly recall our first conversation about a copy that ignited her passion for writing a book.

This mesmerizing tale unfolds the story of two individuals navigating a love affair in the digital age, transcending screens into realms of romance and suspense. Pratichi's storytelling skill invites readers to delve into the intricate connections between the digital and real worlds.

As you turn each page, the boundaries between romance and suspense blur, weaving a tapestry of emotions beyond the realms of the virtual and tangible.

As we embark on this journey, let yourself be captivated by the magic Pratichi weaves. Each heart emoji conceals a secret, and every click takes you deeper into a love story resonating with the unpredictable rhythm of life.

Witnessing her book launch is a proud moment for me, as she truly deserves this success.

– Priya Guleria

Acknowledgments

Embarking on the journey of my second book has been nothing short of an exhilarating odyssey, and I'm thrilled to extend my gratitude to those who made it possible.

A heartfelt shoutout to my family—mom, dad, and my rockstar sisters Himani and Nimisha Sanaye, my in-laws —for their unwavering support. Special thanks to my aunts, uncles, and everyone who's been my pillar of strength. Love you all!

Big thanks to Vishal Kanade for being my writing comrade and navigating the imperfections; he made me write flawlessly and dedicated endless hours to perfecting every word and standing by me through thick and thin. You're the real MVP!

Dedicated to our adorable Simba, your playful spirit inspired every word on these pages. Thank you for being my constant joy.

Gulraj Bedi, you're a script wizard! Your endless reviews helped me smooth out all the kinks. Cheers to your brilliance!

To God, thanks for being on my side.

To my readers, thank you for taking this literary journey with me. Your enthusiasm and feedback are the driving forces that keep my pen moving.

I sincerely thank the dedicated team at Notion Press, who played a crucial role in bringing this book from manuscript to reality. Your professionalism and commitment to the craft are truly commendable.

Lastly, to the countless cups of coffee, moments of self-doubt, and joyous breakthroughs—thank you for being integral parts of this creative process.

This book is a product of collective effort and shared passion, and I am fortunate to be surrounded by such an inspiring and supportive community. Here's to the joy of storytelling and the boundless possibilities of imagination.

A special shoutout to Srujana Dhuri for lending her unique perspective to my book. Thanks for adding that extra spice!

Chapter 1

Online Dating is a Headache!

The morning sunlight filtered through the curtains, casting a soft glow on my untidy room. The echoes of an epic-scale argument from a turbulent night with my father still lingered in the air. Rubbing the sleep from my eyes, I groggily made my way to the bathroom. The cool tiles beneath my feet provided a momentary respite as I tried to shake off the emotional residue of the previous night. In the mirror, my reflection seemed to carry the weight of the unresolved conflict.

After the brief interlude in the bathroom, I emerged, hoping for a sense of normalcy. The world outside awaited, but before venturing into the day, I reached for my phone to gauge the aftermath of the emotional storm that had passed.

There were several missed calls and messages from my father that I ignored. As I scrolled through my phone's notification window, 15 missed calls, and a few messages from Sarah greeted me.

Sarah: Hi, where are you?

Meet me in 2 hours

Near Airport Term. 1.

Hey, you there?

Speak up, chummy!!!!!!

Have you died or what???

Me: Hey babe, sorry. I was asleep.😟

Sarah: Huh? What time is it? Where the hell are you? Just screw everything and come n meet me!

Me: "When?

Sarah: In half an hour, get ready and meet up!

Me: okay. But where??

Sarah: Near Terminal 1, IGI Airport (Metro Station)

Me: I would need some time. I'm still in bed.😳

Sarah: STFU and meet me ASAP. You are already late!

It was 11.30 am when I rushed to the bathroom to take a quick shower. My hair was a total mess. Well, that is because I had not showered for three days. The marks on my breast, while I was taking a shower, reminded me of the time I had spent with Aarav. We had been together for three years before he decided to ruin our relationship. Sarah and I had been friends for eight years.

Like all humans, Sarah wasn't perfect, but she was devoted. She was my best friend. I'd run into her at school. We were in fifth grade at that time. We both had one thing in common: neither of us had a mother. Sarah and I were poles apart. I, for one, believed in old-school love. Love, according to me, has nothing to do with sharing the same bed. Love, as I see it, is something profoundly fragile but beautiful. Many might disagree, but I strongly believe that true love is like fine wine.

It takes several years to concoct the finest of wines. Allow me to quote Kitty Thomas, the author who wrote *The Last Girl*, 2012

"You can't fall in love that fast. Not real love. Real love takes time, like a fine wine. Real love takes years. Not days. Not weeks."

Sarah, on the other hand, had a taste for relationships with no strings attached... She held the infamous distinction of dating five guys simultaneously. The whole of our school knew of Sarah's dating adventures, but nobody had the courage to confront her, thanks to her father's influence, who happened to be Richie Rich.

After chatting with Sarah for a while, I had a bath, got ready and took my scooter in order to meet Sarah. I made my way to Terminal 1: IGI Airport. It took me more than an hour to reach my destination.

Sarah was waiting for me outside the metro station, and as I parked the scooter, she teasingly exclaimed, "My dear Vixen, you are late, as always!"

Hugging me sweetly, she suggested, "Let's go and eat something. I am famished."

We decided on a nearby cafe known for its great coffee and wraps. As we settled in, I stirred sugar into my coffee and inquired, "So, what's up? Why are we meeting so early?"

Sarah, looking concerned, replied, "Nothing, I just wanted to meet you. You haven't been responding to my messages."

"Yeah, I just had a heated argument with my father," I admitted, the tension of the conversation still fresh in my mind.

"What happened? Is everything okay?" Sarah asked, leaning in.

"Yeah, it's just that my dad is a bit stubborn. He wants me to travel to Germany and study at the Munich Business School," I explained.

"Well, what's so bad about it? Munich is a beautiful city. I, for one, would have relished the opportunity." Sarah shared her perspective.

"I don't want to travel abroad at this point. I just wish to complete my education here. After that, I'd start exploring the world. Besides, I don't want to leave him alone. After all, he is the only family I have." I confided.

Sarah empathized, "Ah, I completely buy your point. Don't worry. These things happen; don't take these arguments to heart."

I nodded in agreement, the weight of loneliness evident in my expression.

"I have been feeling lonely, Sarah. I have been feeling an immense weight on my shoulders ever since I ceased contact with Aarav." I confessed, my tone filled with solemnity and pain.

Quick to cheer me up, Sarah reminded me of the good times we had shared.

"Oh, Aaditi, you don't have to feel sad. Remember all the amazing times we have spent over all these years. The laughs we have shared and the triumphs we have enjoyed. Remember the time when you and I stuck together after some seniors from our school began stalking you on Facebook? One of them shared a picture of his erect penis with you. We were quick to file a complaint with the cyber cell." Sarah reminisced.

"Yes, Sarah. It was very uncomfortable when those seniors started sharing inappropriate messages. You were the one who stayed with me throughout the ordeal. You have always been a pillar of strength, and I want you to know that I am grateful." I acknowledged.

"Chill, Aaditi. We are best friends, and that is the least I could have done for you. Now, listen to me. You don't need Aarav anymore. There are other amazing guys you can get along with," Sarah reassured me with a mischievous smile. She then asked for my phone, saying, "Let me find a guy for you." and proceeded to download Tinder.

"Aaditi, have you given any thought to getting back into the dating game?" she asked, her enthusiasm evident.

"Sarah, you know that the entire experience left me feeling a bit shaken. I am not quite sure if I am ready to dive into the world of online dating just yet." I hesitated.

"Honey, I know why you are uncomfortable. However, you can't keep living in the past. There are plenty of gentlemen who are willing to accept you. Besides, you need to regain your confidence, and getting back out there might just be the thing you need to regain your self-confidence and self-esteem." Sarah urged.

"You are correct, my dear friend, but it would be difficult for me to trust anybody. However, I will give it a try if you insist," I agreed.

"The time is ripe for you to embrace the wonders of technology. Haven't you heard of Tinder?" Sarah questioned, her excitement palpable.

"Yes, I have heard of it, but I haven't used it. Isn't it meant for finding casual hookups?" I inquired.

"Well, that is just a part of it. I use it as a platform to meet new people. This platform can be of immense help if you wish to find meaningful connections. According to me, it's quite similar to a treasure hunt, albeit virtual," Sarah explained.

"I guess I could give it a shot. However, I am a bit hesitant about meeting someone online. What if I come across someone using a fake profile?" I expressed my concerns.

"I do get your concerns, Aaditi, but you're wiser now. You know how to dodge all the red flags out there, don't you? Moreover, do not settle for anything less than respect. Plus, you have me by your side if anything goes wrong." Sarah assured.

"Alright. I will give it a try." I conceded.

"Sure thing! No more jerks! Just swipe left without a second thought. Now, let's get you ready for the world of Tinder. Share a few hot pictures of yourself. Let this be the beginning of a fresh new chapter." Sarah encouraged, bringing a sense of excitement to the prospect of a new beginning.

I smiled while feeling a mixture of nervousness and excitement. As I sipped my coffee and listened to Sarah's enthusiastic advice, I couldn't help but feel a glimmer of hope. Maybe someone out there was willing to treat me with love and kindness. I was ready to take that leap of faith and embrace whatever adventures awaited me.

We finished our food. I hugged Sarah before making my way to the parking area where I had parked my scooter. Sarah accompanied me. "You have to be optimistic, Aaditi. You can't let your past define you. One bad experience should not hold you back. Life is all about learning from your experiences and getting better."

I smiled at Sarah and waved her goodbye.

_______Sarah's perspective__________

Her father called her an enchanting beauty. Aaditi embodied a life of privilege because she was a daddy's girl. Ornamenting her life was a symbol of luxury, elegance and indulgence. Every aspect of her lifestyle reflected adoration and wealth.

From a young age, her stunning features captivated all who laid eyes upon her. She had a pair of radiant eyes that twinkled like the stars. Her eyes possessed a natural allure that made her unique in a crowd of millions. Plus, her smile could melt even the coldest and unkind of hearts. However, her physical beauty was merely a prelude to the depth of her character & the generosity that defined her soul.

Aaditi enjoyed an extraordinary bond with her father. He showered all of the world's luxuries upon her. He nurtured her with love and instilled a sense of self-worth in her. Consequently, she grew up believing in her inherent value. Her dad's unwavering support played a great part in shaping her outlook on life. It was her father's support that helped foster a confident & compassionate spirit.

Aaditi was spoiled with love & affection. She enjoyed a lifestyle wherein no desire went unfulfilled. As surprising as it might sound, amidst the trappings of luxury, Aaditi's heart remained grounded in humility and kindness. She had been quick to realize that her privileged position in life made it possible for her to make a positive impact on others. Aaditi and I devoted ourselves to charitable endeavors. She worked extensively to uplift the children at an NGO in Connaught Place. She shared a special bond with the underprivileged. She and her dad ran a school for the underprivileged in Gurgaon.

It goes without saying that money provided her with all of the world's material comforts. However, Aaditi found true joy in the relationships she nurtured. Her circle of friends encompassed people from all walks of life. All of her close friends, including myself, admired her authenticity. It was her willingness to step out of her comfort zone to help others that helped give rise to friendships that withstood the test of time.

In my opinion, Aaditi is the epitome of grace and kindness, and she continues to inspire me with her commitment and dedication. In a world marred by divisiveness and betrayal, her presence is a reminder that true beauty lies not just in physical appearance but also in a person's capacity to touch lives and leave an everlasting imprint of generosity and compassion. However, she has always been emotionally sensitive when it comes to her mother. Losing her at a young age due to health issues had a profound impact on her. As a result, her relationship with her father became even stronger since he became her primary source of love and support.

Aaditi Reaches Home After Meeting Sarah

That night, I finally took Sarah's suggestions into consideration and decided to give Tinder a try. I could feel a wave of nervousness engulfing me. I took a deep breath and decided to dive into the unknown.

At first, I came across so many profiles that seemed too good to be genuine. Some of the profiles appeared fake and superficial, with images of cats and dogs ornamenting them.

To put things simply, I clearly wasn't the one for flings. Well, I felt flings were redundant. Sleeping with someone just for the sake of pleasure sounds 'gross'. Well, call me old-fashioned, but that is me.

Just as I was thinking this, among the sea of profiles, I came across the profile of a guy named Zayn. Something about his profile and bio ended up catching my attention. A genuine smile seemed to light up his face, and his interests aligned with mine. I felt like a breath of fresh air compared to all the other profiles I had come across.

With a surge of curiosity, I swiped right and hoped for a match. To my surprise, it happened within minutes. Zayn and I matched, creating a spark of enthusiasm within my soul. Within no time, I was messaging him on Tinder. I was pleasantly surprised by his witty and frank conversation. As we dove deeper into our mutual interests, discovering common passions of movies, music and travel, I realized that Zayn was easy to get along with. The more we talked, the more I felt that Zayn had a genuine depth to him.

Zayn seemed a fascinating guy with a unique combination of interests and talents. As he was a huge Salman Khan fan, he knew all of the dialogues from Salman's movies by heart. Zayn was not just a passive fan but an active participant in the world of cinema. He was a true movie buff, always up to date with the latest releases, and loved discussing and analyzing films with his friends.

What set Zayn apart was his talent for creating memes. He had an impeccable sense of humor and a knack for finding the perfect quotes, images, and video clips to create hilarious and relatable memes. His friends often looked up to him for a good laugh, and he never disappointed them. This is something he told me during our candid conversations. I, too, could realize that Zayn was good at creating memes and jokes.

His Facebook profile, a link to which was available on Tinder, contained several memes. Most of the content he created was packed with famous Bollywood dialogues. To be honest, It was his ability to make people laugh that made him look attractive.

Zayn and I kept talking to each other for a week. After a week of exchanging messages, Zayn suggested that we meet in person. He, too, was a Delhiite and lived near the Rajiv Chowk.

At first, the both of us decided to meet at a mall. It felt like a casual and comfortable setting, providing us both with an opportunity to ease into the new chapter. However, he asked me If we could watch a movie instead. We decided to watch 'Prem Ratan Dhan Payo'.

I told him that I'd be traveling to Connaught Place. So, he booked two movie tickets for Sunday afternoon. A part of me was nervous and hesitant, I must confess.

The memories of my relationship with Aarav kept tormenting me. However, I could not deny the connection I had established with Zayn through our conversations. I decided to trust my instincts and agreed to meet him.

As I prepared for the date, I couldn't help but experience a mix of excitement and thrill. Could it be the beginning of something special? Or will it be a learning curve in my dating journey? Well, only time knows the answer.

I was hopeful but also aware of the uncertainties of online dating. I was all prepared to approach this meeting with an open heart and a cautious mind. I was willing to enjoy the experience, regardless of the outcome.

However, all of my excitement and optimism died a slow and painful death.

I don't have words to describe the rollercoaster of emotions I went through after my disastrous date with Zayn. It felt like a nightmare, and I have struggled to get it out of my head. I wanted to pour my heart and frustrations into a diary, hoping it would provide me with peace and strength.

The day of my movie date with Zayn dawned upon me. My heart was pounding with apprehension. I bought a gift for him, a pair of AirPods. Also, I asked my driver to drop me off. He has been working for my father for over a decade now. He is a bit overprotective but treats me like his own daughter. Also, I asked him to keep my meeting with Zayn a secret. I didn't want my father to know anything about it. Well, I am a girl who enjoys keeping secrets.

The traffic was at its peak. Therefore, I decided to message Zayn in order to inform him that I'd be late. This is how our conversation went:

Me: Hi, Zayn. Sorry 2 inform u of this, but I think I'd be late. There's a lot of traffic here.☹

Zayn: Fuck. Make it quick. The movie is about to start.

I asked the driver to drive as quickly as he possibly could. We did end up jumping a few red lights in the process.

When I reached the Odeon, I saw Zayn waiting for me at the entrance. He looked just as handsome as his pictures, but there was something about the way he carried himself that gave me a tinge of arrogance. I wanted to shake his hand, but he bluntly refused.

Zayn had a somewhat shady attitude. He came across as carefree and laid-back. There was always a sense of mystery surrounding his actions and intentions. It was hard to predict what he was going to do next.

The both of us settled into our seats. The anticipation was building as the lights dimmed. But from the very beginning of 'Prem Ratan Dhan Payo', it was very clear that Zayn was not the Prince Charming I was searching for. He began yelling at the screen, cracking crude jokes and making vulgar gestures.

He said, "You know what, Sonam Kapoor is hot. She is too hot for Sallu Bhai. I wish I could fuck her."

That was disgusting. I thought, "That's gross, Zayn. How can you even think of saying that in an auditorium filled with people?"

He replied rudely, "Right! So, forget about Sonam Kapoor. Let me fuck you first. Young girls want one thing, i.e. cock. Do you want to see mine? I have fucked ten girls in the last six months. They all love my cock. Would you like to taste it?"

However, things did not stop there. His behavior only grew worse as the movie progressed. He leaned closer, invading my personal space, and asked me to unzip his trousers. I was mortified, to say the least. How could someone be so disrespectful? I could feel my face burning with embarrassment, and a part of me wanted to run away from that suffocating situation.

As I glanced around the auditorium, I noticed the disapproving glares from those around us. I could even feel the weight of their judgment. I couldn't muster the courage to bear his crude antics. I summoned all of my strength and decided to walk out of the auditorium. The look of bewilderment on Zayn's face was both satisfying and disheartening.

While walking out of the multiplex, I felt a barrage of emotions overpowering me, right from relief to anger and everything in between. I had put myself out there, hoping for a meaningful and respectful meeting. However, I was confronted with such disrespect and objectification. My trust had been shattered into a million pieces.

As I sit here, pouring my heart out to you, I wish to remind myself of all the lessons I have learned. I wish to hold onto my self-respect and self-worth. I do not wish to settle for anything less than respect and mutual understanding. Nobody deserves to be treated the way Zayn treated me, and I won't let this horrendous experience define my future.

I promised myself that I would trust my instincts and value my own well-being. I won't let the actions of a jerk overshadow my belief in love and togetherness. I do hope that by sharing my story, others will find inspiration and strength to stand up against mistreatment.

I was quick to text Sarah after I had reached home. I wanted to yell at her but reminded myself that she was my best friend.

Me: Sarah, you moron. You made me download Tinder. You won't believe what happened. I went on a date with that guy Zayn from Tinder, and it was a complete disaster!!!!! 😐

Sarah: Calm Down! What happened, babe?😅

Me: This Tinder date was a disaster! We went to watch Prem Ratan Dhan Payo. He kept making vulgar gestures. I was scared. Everyone was judging us in that theater.😢

Sarah: That is just so gross!!! I'm sorry you had to go through all of this, sweetie!😑

Me: It got bad. He was worse than just gross. That fucker wanted me to jerk him off on our 1st date. Can you imagine?😫

Sarah: This cannot be accepted. How could he behave like that in public? It's so horrendous. I can't believe you had to witness it.😳

Me; I could not believe my eyes either. This guy had no filter and no regard for anybody else's comfort. I felt trapped.

Sarah: I'm sorry, Aaditi. Nobody should have to endure such tribulation. It's not your fault.

Me: Thanks for your support. I'm just disappointed. I thought Zayn could be different, but I was wrong. He was a jerk!!!

Sarah: You deserve much better, Aaditi. Don't let this bad experience get to your head. You will find someone who cares for you.

Me: Yeah, right, I am deleting this Tinder crap.

Sarah: Are. Don't do that. You will get a better match next. You never know!

Me: Whatever! Talk later!

I reached home and decided to take a shower. It had been a tough afternoon, and I needed to relax. I took a hot shower and asked my cook to prepare coffee.

As I sipped my coffee and relaxed, I received an email. My heart skipped a beat as I saw this email notification pop up on my phone. It was Aarav, my ex-boyfriend. I had not spoken to him ever since I joined college.

A part of me wanted to ignore the email, to keep the past in the past and move forward. After all, I had worked so hard to heal and find my own happiness after the break-up. However, there was a part of me that couldn't help but wonder, 'What if?'

What if Aarav had changed? What if he wanted to apologize for the pain he had caused? What if there was a chance to make amends? All of these what-ifs kept floating in my head. I found myself torn between caution and a lingering curiosity.

I stared at the email with my fingers hovering over the keyboard. I was unsure of how to respond. Well, that is because memories of our tumultuous relationship kept flashing before my eyes. These memories reminded me of the heartache and betrayal I had gone through. It had taken me so long to rebuild my self-esteem and muster the courage to move on.

As I pondered, I realized that I had grown a great deal since my break-up. I was no longer the broken, vulnerable girl I once was. I had been able to rediscover my self-reliance after the break-up. I had decided to pursue my passion. Thankfully, I had a small but reliable network of supportive friends like Sarah to fall back on. I had become stronger and more resilient.

However, as the evening unfolded, I continued to think of Aarav. Several memories from my past began overpowering me.

The next morning, an unexpected surprise arrived: an unnamed gift. A delicate and beautiful bracelet adorned with intricate charms. It lay nested in a box on my doorstep. My maid was the first person to see the box.

I held the bracelet in my hands, marveling at its craftsmanship. As my heart raced, I pondered over the sender's identity. I was sure that Aarav could have been the one responsible for the present. I kept thinking that maybe he wanted to entice me back into his web. I remembered how he liked to play mind games. The bracelet seemed to be a piece of the jigsaw in his complex game, an emblem of his ego.

Despite the unease that had settled in, I found happiness in my friendship with Sarah. I messaged her and told her about the bracelet. Our conversation led me to revisit the labyrinth of emotions I had locked away. I took my phone and pinged Sarah.

Me: Sarah, See this.

I sent her a picture of a bracelet.

Sarah: Stunning! It's so pretty. Did your dad give it to you?

Me: I got a parcel this morning

Sarah: What parcel?

Me: This bracelet. I think Aarav sent it😫

Sarah: Aarav, that egoistic freak? What makes you think so?

Me: He messaged me this morning😓

Sarah: Let us meet and discuss this.

A bad memory that I had buried ages ago had begun resurfacing, and I didn't know how to bury it again.

Chapter 2

The Woman I Have Become

Moving on is tough, isn't it? I say this because loving someone deeply is bound to make you feel vulnerable. I remember meeting Aarav, a handsome hunk, at school. He was the perfect physical specimen: tall, slender, and fit. Also, the sight of his rippling muscles was the one to behold. I had met him during one of my school trips to the Corbett National Park, and we had both started dating. It was love at first sight.

I also remember bunking a class to be with Aarav. I was in class 9. At school, he was my senior, and we spent a lot of time together. However, all good things come to an end, don't they?

Some of my life's finest moments hovered around Aarav, but he was no longer there by my side, and that was the hardest part.

"I want to be with you for the rest of my life," I told him once while roaming the Sarojini Nagar market.

"Me, too, want to be with you for the rest of my life," he had replied.

The two of us studied together. Well, 'studying' was just an excuse. We were both quite attracted physically, though I never wanted to cross that line. During one of our meetings at

the ever-popular market, the both of us had confessed our love for each other.

Well, we were teenagers, naive and innocent, but there was absolute truth in what we had conveyed. The message was clear. It was at this moment that Aarav held my hand and took me to a secluded corner. Well, it is difficult to find a peaceful corner in Nagar. The market is always buzzing with shopaholics.

The both of us went into the car park. It was there that Aarav kissed me for the first time. I was 15 at that time, while he was 17. I could feel the shivers that were concocted the moment our lips met.

Unsurprisingly, our liplock gave rise to something more streamy and sensuous. Aarav asked me to sit in the car. He was 17, but no policeman in Delhi had the courage to stop him or question him. Well, rumor had it that Aarav's father had pocketed some of the high-ranking police officers. Actually, Aarav's father was building a residential complex, and several high-ranking officials were to get a flat of their own. The land on which the housing project was being built had been acquired after an 'under-the-table' arrangement between several high-ranking officials. The political people were involved as well.

Well, my apologies for getting zoned out.

So, we began craving for each other after we broke the liplock. A few minutes later, Aarav took me to his home in

Hauz Khas. His parents weren't home. His mother had gone to Shirdi while his father was away on business. So, the two of us made our way into his bedroom. I was pretty nervous. It is not that I did not want to have sex. I was nervous because I was scared of the pain that accompanies it.

So, Aarav was all ready to take my virginity. He approached me and began kissing me.

"You ready to get humped?" he asked in the naughtiest of voices.

I didn't say anything. All I gave him was a nod. He unbuttoned my shirt and began touching my breasts. He removed my shirt and began sliding his hand inside my bra.

"Your breasts are soft and tender. Have you ever had sex?" He asked.

"No, I haven't." I replied. Out of nowhere, He removed my bra and began kissing my breasts. He made me lie down and began eating my breasts. He appeared excited, much like a 5-year-old feasting upon his favorite ice cream cone. A few lustful moans escaped my lips. The experience was novel, and I wanted it to continue. He bit my breasts, and I couldn't help myself. The pain and the pleasure were immense. I hadn't experienced anything of this sort in my life ever before. My vagina began throbbing, he slid his hand inside my skirt and began teasing me. He inserted one of his fingers inside my vagina, and I began moaning. A couple of minutes later, his fingers began moving rhythmically. The experience became pleasurable.

He unbuttons his pants and takes my hand over his dick. He asked me to give it a stroke, and I gripped it tight. I could feel his dick getting harder and harder. And at that moment, he asked me to sit down and take his dick in his mouth. I was a bit uncomfortable as I had never experienced it. Aarav was quite excited to do so, but the moment I took it in my mouth, he became an animal. And that made me feel sick. He began choking me with both his hands. I could not breathe. I mustered enough courage to ask him to stop (at once).

I told him to stop right there.

"Aarav, I don't think we should be doing this. I am just not comfortable." I got up, adjusted my clothes, and ran as fast as I could. Aarav looked at me, baffled, as I exited the room. There was displeasure in his eyes.

I kept thinking of the time I had spent with Aarav. This thought broke when Sarah called me.

I answered Sarah's call and asked her to meet me near the 'Khan Chacha' outlet. The chicken tikka roll they serve is just sumptuous. It is our favorite spot.

Just as I was about to leave my house, I received a message on Tinder. At first, I decided to ignore it.

"Where are you going?" asked my maid as she was preparing breakfast.

"I have to reach college before 11 am, Aunty. I am already running late." I replied.

"What about breakfast, beta?" she asked.

"Pack it and give it to me." I replied.

I got my breakfast packed and made my way to Khan Market. I asked Driver Dada (my driver) to drive as fast as he possibly could.

"Traffic bahot hai mam. Main tezz kaise chalaaun?" (There's too much traffic, ma'am. How do you expect me to speed up?) he asked.

I kept quiet. I got stuck in traffic near the Flyover at Janak Puri. Along the way, I offered my breakfast to a poor and hungry kid. She gave a big smile. The look on her face told a story.

I was quick to message Sarah and inform her that I'm running late. Long pops of notifications greeted me as I checked my phone. A guy named Vedh had messaged me on Tinder.

"Hi, I am Vedh. Just came across your profile. Can we talk whenever you are free?" He had messaged.

I did not care to respond to his message. Well, I wanted to delete Tinder because my experience of finding a date online had been catastrophic. However, I didn't do it immediately. I wanted to have a chat with Sarah regarding this. I ignored the message Vedh had sent before stuffing the phone into my pocket.

I reached my destination and messaged Sarah to meet me at the Khan Chacha outlet. To my surprise, she was already there. She had ordered my favorite roll, which was the Chicken Malai Tikka Roll.

She collected the order and began walking toward me.

"Hey, Sarah! Sorry, I'm late. The traffic was absolutely nuts."

"Oh, I get it. It felt like you'd never make it. What else happened?" Sarah inquired, her curiosity evident.

"Sincerely, it was like the entire city decided to hit the roads simultaneously. Anyway, how's your day been?" I asked, attempting to shift the focus.

"Same old, same old. Exam prep is driving me crazy. So, spill the beans. How's life treating you?"

"Not too shabby, considering the usual chaos," I replied with a nonchalant shrug. "Speaking of crazy, remember I mentioned my worst date ever? Well, it was with Zayn."

She empathetically responded, "Oh yeah! I am so sorry to hear that, ya. Online dating can be tough, and it's unfortunate, but don't worry, there's someone out there who'll be a perfect match for you."

"I hope so, Sarah. It's quite disheartening when all I can get is disappointments," I sighed.

She's being the supportive friend as always was, suggested, "I understand how you feel, but hey, I have an idea. Why don't you come to my birthday party? It won't be like any typical party, and who knows, you might meet someone cool and amazing at my birthday party."

"Hmmm. I am not sure, Sarah. I am really not in the mood for socializing right now. That bracelet sent by Aarav has also caught me by surprise. I thought I had left my memories with Aarav behind me."

"What's with the bracelet? Did you talk to Aarav about it?" She inquired with genuine concern.

"No, I did not. An email came this morning. It was Aarav. He said he wanted to get things right. A parcel came about an hour after I saw the email."

"Are you going to talk to Aarav about this?" She asked, sensing the complexity of the situation.

"No. Not at all! He is an egoistic bastard. You know what? I don't want to talk about that freak. I have had enough of his nonsense. Let's not talk about him anymore," I declared, firm in my decision.

"As you say, babe. Now, let's find another date for you," She suggested, attempting to shift the focus.

"I said I am not in the mood to socialize right now."

"Come on, Aaditi, trust me. It will be different. You know me, and I genuinely want you to be there. You're my bestie."

"Sarah, I will surely be coming to the party, but I don't want to date someone right now."

"That is alright! As you say, babe. Also, I promise it'll be a memorable evening..." Sarah assured, trying to inject a sense of excitement into my hesitant heart.

I was eagerly waiting for Sarah's birthday. Well, you can say that I wished to keep all of the negativity aside by keeping myself busy. Also, I wanted to throw Aarav out of my life. I hoped that staying close to her would protect me from Aarav's wickedness.

She would get him arrested within no time if he acted smart. Sarah was a girl who hated cringe talks. She had a history of getting stalkers and bullies arrested. Besides, she could do anything in order to protect me. She loved me, pretty much like a sister, and my happiness was of paramount importance to her.

I was thrilled when the day of the party finally arrived. I had spent hours searching for the perfect gift for Sarah, and I settled on a personalized bracelet with her initials. As soon as I arrived at the party, I was immediately drawn to Sarah's vibrant energy. We laughed, danced, and enjoyed each other's company. It was a night filled with joy and celebration, and I felt lucky to be a part of it. She wore a beautiful red dress.

She hugged me and asked me to join her for a drink. Some of the city's wealthiest 'kids' were there at the party. One of Punjabi Bagh's finest bars was hosting the party. Plus, Sarah loved spending big bucks on parties and get-togethers, all thanks to her family background.

As the party progressed, Sarah's attention began to drift away from me. She was a gracious host, and understandably, she was required to attend to other guests as well. I found myself feeling a bit left out, surrounded by unfamiliar faces and conversations.

In the midst of my discomfort, I noticed Vikram, a friend of Sarah's (and a womanizer), making his way toward me. He had always been charming, but tonight, his flirtatious demeanor was too much for me to handle. He brought me a drink, which I accepted. Soon enough, his sinister plans started coming to light. He made me drink four glasses of wine. I was intoxicated, Vikram. "You look hot! Wanna have a one-night stand?"

I told him, "Stop it, Vikram!"

"You are the juiciest chick out here. You belong in my bed. Wanna have a nice hanky-panky session with me?" he said while caressing my thighs.

"Hahah! Shut up, you fucker!" I was too intoxicated. However, I hadn't lost my mind. I got up from there. I don't understand why Sarah had invited this dumbfuck.

With a racing heart and a fake smile, I excused myself politely, passing a bunch of other groups. I quickly made my way through the crowd, navigating through laughter and conversations, hoping to find solace outside.

Once I reached the quiet solitude of the outdoors, I took a deep breath, letting the cool evening air wash away my anxiety and discomfort. I reminded myself that I deserved to feel comfortable and respected in any situation. I decided to leave the party, realizing that my mental well-being was more important to me than any social obligation.

I felt a mixture of relief, rage, and frustration as I left the location. I was hoping for a memorable night with Sarah, so I had been looking forward to it. But things had taken an unexpected turn, and I was reminded how important it is to set limits and put my comfort first.

I called my driver uncle and decided to enjoy a lavish meal (all by myself). On the way, I thought of forgetting the ordeal. Just then, I realized that a guy named Vedh had messaged me a couple of days ago. I decided to respond (out of sheer curiosity). I opened the app and typed him a message.

Me: Hey Vedh, just saw your message! What's up!😊

It took Vedh just about ten minutes to respond.

Vedh: Your reply was quick! I was literally waiting for almost two days now. But you know, it's worth the wait! 😄

Me: Haha, sorry about that! My life decided to go on a crazy rollercoaster. But hey, better late than never, right?😜

Vedh: Late, but definitely worth it. Life can be a wild ride; glad you hopped on this conversation coaster! By the way, you've got some cute dimples there. 😊

Me:(Blushes) Aw, thanks! They make an appearance when I least expect it.😋

Vedh: Well, consider me pleasantly surprised then. You're making me smile here. So, spill the beans—how many hearts have those dimples stolen so far?😍

Me: Oh, you know, a few here and there. But the real question is, how many dimples does it take to win your heart?😉

Vedh: Smooth! I'd say just one, but I'm willing to be convinced otherwise.😘

Me: Well, a charmer like you must have left a trail of hearts yourself. How's your dating history looking?😇

Vedh: Oh, you know, a few tales to tell. But here I am, still swiping left and right, but nothing as captivating as the mystery behind those dimples. Yours must have a few interesting chapters, too.😉

Me: Same here! The dating scene is like a maze, and I'm just trying not to get lost. Fingers crossed for a happy ending, though.🙄

Vedh: With a guide like you, I'd happily get lost in the maze. Who knows, we might find a happy ending together. By the way, since we're on the topic of mysteries, what's your horoscope? I'm a Gemini.😛

Me: I'm a Pisces! I've heard Pisces and Gemini aren't the best match. What's your take on that?😮

Vedh: Oh, the classic horoscope drama! They say we're not the best match, but I think we can defy the stars, don't you? 🤪

Me: Haha Definitely! Who needs a perfect match when you can have a perfectly entertaining mismatch? 😄

Vedh: Mismatch, match, as long as it's with you, it's perfect. Let's make our own constellation of laughter and see where it takes us. 😂

Me: I like the way you think, Vedh! Laughter is the best way to navigate through the cosmic chaos. 🚀

Vedh: Glad you're on board! Get ready for a journey full of laughs and maybe a few unexpected twists. 🌀

Me: I'm all in! The more unexpected, the better. Let the cosmic adventure begin! 🚀😄

I've had fun chatting with Vedh on Tinder for a while now, and our connection has been nothing short of delightful. After some witty banter and playful exchanges on the app, we decided to take our conversation to a more personal level and exchanged numbers, moving things over to WhatsApp. He is not only genuinely funny but also incredibly flattering with his compliments. His pickup lines had me in stitches, and we found ourselves speaking well into the early hours of the morning. It's been a refreshing and fun experience getting to know him—a guy who is not only charming but also down-to-earth and authentic. Vedh's humor and warmth have added a special touch to our interactions.

Two weeks later...

Within no time, my conversations with Vedh began gathering steam. However, a part of me was hesitant. Well, that is because I hardly knew Vedh. We had met online, and while our conversations had been enjoyable, there was still that nagging uncertainty lingering at the back of my mind.

I scrolled through our WhatsApp conversation, reading our lighthearted exchanges. A part of me wanted to believe that Vedh was genuine. His words were comforting, and he seemed to genuinely care about my well-being. However, I could not help but wonder if it was all too good to be true.

Past experiences have taught me to be cautious and not let myself be easily swayed by the charm of someone new. I had been hurt before, and the wounds were still healing. Opening up to someone again felt like stepping on fragile ground, unsure of the outcome.

However, there was something about Vedh's presence that made me want to take a bold move. His positive outlook on life, his adventurous spirit, and the way he listened to my concerns made me feel understood. Maybe, just maybe, he was different.

Yet, doubts continued to plague my mind. How could I be certain that he wasn't just putting on a facade? The world of online connections could be deceiving; after all, images and words on a screen could hide a multitude of truths.

I decided to take a deep breath. Furthermore, I wanted to remind myself to trust my instincts. I hadn't sensed any red flags in our conversations thus far. Vedh had been patient, kind, and supportive, providing me with ample space to express my emotions without judgment. However, he hadn't shared his own experiences, his victories, and his vulnerabilities. Well, it was just the beginning.

Maybe it was time to let go of my skepticism and give Vedh a chance. After all, building trust requires taking risks. I could not let past heartbreak define my future interactions. Life is all about taking chances, stepping into the unknown, and allowing oneself to be vulnerable.

With newfound determination, I picked up my phone and typed out a message to Vedh. I thanked him for being there lately. I did express my hesitations but assured him that I was willing to take a leap of faith, hoping that he would prove to be the person he portrayed himself to be.

As I pressed the send button, a mix of nervousness and excitement washed over me. Only time could reveal whether trusting Vedh was the right decision. I had decided to embrace the uncertainty.

Vedh and I started texting almost every day now.

Me: Hey Vedh! How's your day going?😁

Vedh: Hey you! It's going pretty well, but it just got a whole lot better now that I'm talking to you. 😉

Me: Aw, you're too sweet! What's making your day so great?

Vedh: Well, I have to admit, talking to someone as amazing as you is definitely a highlight. 😏

Me: Haha, stop it! You're going to make me blush. So, any exciting plans for the weekend?

Vedh: Hmm, I was thinking about spending it with someone special. Any chance you're free?

Me: Oh, really now? I might have to check my busy schedule... 😉 *What did you have in mind?*

Vedh: Maybe a dinner and some good conversation? I hear that's the perfect way to spend time with someone you're interested in.

Me: That sounds tempting! I'm always up for good food and company. What's your idea of the perfect dinner?

Vedh: Well, it would involve great company, delicious food, and just the right amount of flirting. How does that sound to you?

Me: Haha, so cheesy!! 😉 Let's make it happen someday soon.

Vedh: How soon, cutie?

Me: Very soon! 😛

Vedh: Awaiting!!! I have a meeting now, Catch up Later?

Me: Sure! Good day!😇

Staring into the mirror, my eyes gleamed with curiosity and determination. The reflection told the story of a woman who'd weathered storms, emerging resilient. My cascading locks spoke of years of cultivating strength through vulnerability.

In my lean form, there existed a delicate balance between body, mind, and spirit. Mastering self-care with a balanced diet and regular exercise, I learned the value of tenacity and the impact of a healthy body on well-being.

Yet, my identity extended beyond the physical. What set me apart was the depth of my character – a bright smile mirroring genuine kindness and love. Sincere relationships brought satisfaction, recognizing the joy in helping others.

Life, to me, wasn't solely about serious introspection. I believed in the healing power of laughter, finding humor in unexpected moments to alleviate life's burdens.

An adventurous spirit burned within, desiring to explore the uncharted territories of the world. Embracing the unknown with open arms, I stepped out of my comfort zone, vowing to make the most of every opportunity.

A new chapter awaited, and with each step, I'd unveil the depths of my being. The pages of my story stood ready, eager to be filled with adventures, triumphs, and the beauty of an authentic, fully-lived life.

Chapter 3
Let Bygones Be Bygones

Rudhay and I have been friends since childhood, sharing a deep bond that goes beyond the current study session. Our fathers have been friends for ages, and the camaraderie between our families has extended to my friendship with Rudhay. Growing up together, we've witnessed each other's milestones and supported one another through various phases of life.

Rudhay possesses a distinct combination of intellect and straightforwardness. With a sharp mind and a knack for grasping complex concepts effortlessly, he stands out as someone inherently smart. His appearance mirrors his no-nonsense attitude, often dressed in clean, minimalist attire that reflects efficiency and focus. Rudhay's sharp features complement his analytical mindset, and his expressive eyes convey a depth of thought. However, his bluntness can sometimes catch others off guard, as he doesn't shy away from expressing his opinions directly. While this honesty can be refreshing, it also adds an intriguing layer to his personality, making interactions with Rudhay both intellectually stimulating and occasionally surprising. Rudhay warmly invited me to his place for a group study session.

Rudhay: Hey there! Thanks for coming over. I've got everything set up in the living room. Let's make the most of our study session!

Me: Of course! I'm glad we're doing this. It's been a while since we've studied together.

[As you both settle in and start studying, Rudhay steers the conversation in an unexpected direction.]

He Said,"You know, I've been thinking about your ex lately. The way he treated you was really crappy. You deserve so much better, someone who appreciates you."

I replied"Yeah, it was tough, but I'm trying to move on and focus on my studies."

He stated, "Absolutely! You need someone who's going to look out for you, someone who genuinely cares."

"Hey, what are you guys talking about?" Alex inquired.

Rudhay responded, "Just discussing how Aaditi deserves someone better than her ex. Someone who'll treat her right."

Understanding the importance of being with someone who values you, Alex shared his perspective.

As the dialogue meandered further into the realm of relationships, I began to feel a growing sense of detachment. In an effort to redirect the conversation, I interjected.

"Thanks for your concern, guys. I appreciate it. But hey, let's get back to our study material. I really want to nail this concept before the exam."

Feeling the need for an escape from the discourse on relationships and parties during our study session, I hastily messaged Vedh, seeking an SOS. My message conveyed, "Hey, Vedh. I need an emergency escape! Can you call me and pretend you need my help with something urgent? I'll pick up and use it as an excuse to leave this boring study group. Thanks a million!"

Anticipation of Vedh's call became my lifeline, a hopeful rescue from the prevailing social scenario.

Rudhay, noticing my distraction, inquired, "Hey, everything alright?"

Glancing at my phone discreetly, I replied, "Actually, I just got a call and realized I have some work I need to take care of."

Curious, He asked, "Oh, really? Anything serious?"

Nodding, I responded, "Yeah, it's a bit urgent. I need to head out."

Rudhay, intrigued, questioned, "What kind of work is it?"

Smiling, I replied, "You know me, I'll fill you in later. It's just one of those unexpected things. Got to run, catch you later!As I quickly gathered my things, I left Rudhay with a sense of curiosity, knowing he'd be itching to ask more questions.

After I left his place, I had a call with Vedh that lasted for about an hour. We delved into a myriad of random topics, exchanging thoughts and banter, often punctuated with laughter. The conversation took a turn toward playful teasing and flirty comments, adding a light and enjoyable vibe to the discussion. It was a welcome contrast to the serious study atmosphere I had just left, and Vedh's witty banter provided a pleasant escape for the evening.

Vedh: (message received) Hey, just wanted to say, you have the cutest voice. It's so soothing. 😊

Me: (replying) Haha, thanks! I appreciate that. What brought that on?

Vedh: (responding) I don't know, just felt like letting you know. Makes me want to cuddle up and chat all night.

Me: (smiling) Well, it's almost bedtime for me. You're lucky you're not here; otherwise, you might have to endure my sleepy rambling.

Vedh: (playfully) I'd take that over silence any day. Sweet dreams, though. 😴

Me: (closing the conversation) Goodnight! Maybe some other time. 😄

Vedh: Goodnight, beautiful! Good luck with your exams!

It was 2 am, and I found myself wide awake with an unfamiliar number persistently calling me. I picked up the call, and it was Aarav's voice I heard. I guess he had switched his number.

"Aaditi! Don't hang up. Please hear me out! Before he could say anything, I hung up the call. I blocked his number again on call logs. But immediately, I got a notification on WhatsApp.

Aarav: I have been doing a lot of thinking lately, and I want to apologize for everything that happened between us. Can we talk and try to make amends?

I read the message, and my emotions conflicted. I took a deep breath before replying. I wanted to shout at him and curse him, but I decided not to lose my composure because Aarav wasn't important to me, not anymore. Arguing with him would be of no use. He was just a bad memory, a nightmare of sorts, and nothing more.

Me: Aarav, I appreciate that you want to make amends, but it is not that simple. You hurt me deeply, and I am not sure if I am ready to forgive and forget just yet.

Aarav: I understand that I messed up, Aaditi, and I can't change the past, but I genuinely want to make things right. I miss you, and I want us to have a chance at rebuilding what we had.

Me: Miss me? After everything that happened? It's not that easy. You broke my trust, and I can't just ignore the pain I went through. Also, that expensive bracelet that you sent is not going to change my perspective of you.

Aarav: I know I made mistakes, but people change. I've learned from my past, and I want to prove that I can be better. Please give me a chance to show you. Also, what bracelet are you talking about?

Me: How can I trust that you won't hurt me again? You had your chances before, and each time, I ended up shattered. I can't go through that again.

Aarav: I understand your hesitation, but we had something special, Aaditi. We can work on it, grow together, and create a stronger bond. I am willing to do whatever it takes.

Me: It's not just about saying the right things. Actions speak louder than words. And right now, your words are echoing the same promises (hollow) you made before.

Aarav: I'm not expecting you to trust me blindly, but can't we at least try? We shared beautiful moments, and I believe we can find our way back to that if we give it a chance.

Me: I wish it were that simple, but trust isn't something that can be repaired overnight. I need ample time and space to heal, to figure out what's best for me.

Aarav: So, you're just going to give up on us? Throw away everything we had because of past mistakes? I thought you were stronger than that.

Me: Don't you dare try to guilt-trip me. This is about self-respect and taking care of my own well-being. I deserve someone who values me and respects my boundaries.

Aarav: Fine, Aaditi. If that is how you feel, then maybe it's best we both move on. Goodbye.

(I read Aarav's final message. I took a moment before composing my response)

Me: Goodbye, Aarav. I hope we both find the happiness we deserve.

Our conversation ended, leaving me with both sadness and relief, knowing that I had made a difficult but necessary decision for my own growth and happiness. I threw the bracelet away. He did not admit that he had sent it, but I knew it was him. I could just feel it.

I had a wave of emotions as I thought back on my relationship with Aarav. I recalled how much I had cherished him and how he had once had a particular place in my heart. I was reminded of the happiness we once enjoyed by the rush of memories from our time together, our laughter, and the dreams we once nourished together.

However, most of these memories were bittersweet, tainted with the hurt of being overlooked. I could think of a number of situations where my efforts and love appeared to be wasted. It seemed more like my efforts in the partnership were expected than valued. Those emotional detachments caused me to doubt my value.

Here's one such instance:

Spring of 2013

I had just cleared class 12. I had scored 93%. So, I wanted to celebrate this with Aarav. I thought of spending some time with him at my place since my dad was not at home. I thought of cooking something special for Aarav. I planned to cook chicken curry since he loved non-vegetarian food. I asked him to come and meet me, but I kept the surprise under wraps.

As I stood in the kitchen, the Aroma of Aarav' favorite dish wafted through the air. It took me close to 90 minutes to cook the traditional Indian Chicken Curry. A mixture of excitement and contentment filled me. The afternoon sun painted a warm glow on the countertops, and I could not help but smile, knowing how much he loved chicken curry.

I had spent hours carefully selecting the ingredients, chopping them with precision, and simmering the gravy to perfection. It was my way of showing how much I cared and how much he meant to me.

My phone buzzed, and I eagerly checked the message. It was Aarav, saying he was coming to see me. I could not wait to see the surprise and delight on his face when he tasted what I had prepared. But as minutes turned into an hour, confusion started to creep in as Aarav was hardly ever late. I sent a quick message, my fingers typing with a mix of excitement and worry.

The reply I got was unexpected, almost dismissive.

"Hey, running late. Meeting up with the guys. Don't wait for me." Those words hit me like a sudden gust of cold wind.

It wasn't just that he was running late; it was the fact that he hadn't thought twice about changing our plans without even letting me know beforehand. The disappointment settled in, heavy and hard to ignore.

I looked at the table I had set so carefully, the plates arranged with precision and the candles casting a soft, flickering light. Everything suddenly felt like it was for naught. The effort, it all felt like it had been taken for granted. My excitement had turned to a dull ache in my chest, a mix of sadness and frustration.

Sitting down at the table alone, I picked at my food, my appetite replaced by a knot of emotions. It wasn't just about the meal; it was about feeling cherished, about knowing that my efforts were seen and appreciated. As I stared at the plate in front of me, I couldn't help but wonder if he ever thought and cared about what I had put into making this evening special.

I deserved that consideration, that acknowledgment. As I navigated the sea of feelings, I hoped that Aarav would come to understand the depth of my emotions beyond the surface of a well-cooked dinner.

Thinking of the plans we had made for our future, I could not help but feel a sense of disappointment. The promises we exchanged, the talks about building a life together, faded into the past, unfulfilled. The potential that once felt limitless had slowly withered away, leaving me wondering how things had turned on their head.

Amidst my reflections, a whirlwind of emotions enveloped me. There was sadness for what we had lost, frustration at myself for allowing the relationship to reach that point, and regret for not recognizing the signs earlier. I often wondered if I should have been more assertive, communicated my feelings more explicitly, or demanded the respect that I deserved.

Through the haze of these feelings, lessons started to emerge. I recognized the importance of self-value, open communication, and setting healthy boundaries. I knew that I deserved a love that reciprocated my efforts and treated me with the appreciation I had always wanted.

In this period of introspection, I understood that healing would take time. Nevertheless, I was determined to move forward. Armed with newfound insights, I was prepared to embark on a journey of growth, self-appreciation, and self-discovery. I was committed to finding a connection built on mutual respect and genuine acknowledgment of each other's feelings.

As I was thinking about all of this, I dozed off.

The day after the exams, Rudhay turned into the Sherlock Holmes of casual conversations. He couldn't resist prying into where I vanished the other day, and what kind of mysterious work appeared out of the blue. Dodging his detective skills, I received a rescue message from Vedh, and like a secret agent receiving a coded message, I got absorbed in my phone. While Rudhay continued his chit-chat with Sarah and the gang, I took cover in Vedh's message, successfully evading the inquisition for the time being.

Vedh: Hey there, beautiful! How are your exams going?

Me: Hey Vedh! Exams are going well. Just surviving the study marathon. Got my last one tomorrow. How about you? Any exciting plans for the day?

Vedh: Ah, the last stretch! You've got this! As for me, just the usual daily chaos. Dinner plans with friends tonight want to join us?

You: Thanks for the encouragement! Dinner sounds great, but I'll be pretty exhausted since the last exam. How about we meet up for a coffee tomorrow in the evening instead?

Vedh: I'm always up for coffee. Evening coffee it is then. Looking forward to it! ☕🌆

Me: Perfect! Coffee is the best post-exam treat. I'll definitely need the caffeine boost. 😄 *See you tomorrow!*

Today has been a whirlwind of emotions and experiences. It all began with the arduous task of preparing for my exams. The days leading up to this moment were filled with countless hours of studying, sleepless nights, and the persistent buzz of academic stress. The thought of meeting Vedh tonight added a unique blend of nerves and excitement, and time seemed to move in slow motion.

The next morning, as the day unfolded and I found myself in the examination hall, I couldn't shake the growing sense of excitement about the evening ahead – a date with Vedh. The very thought had my heart racing and my mind wandering from calculations to our impending meeting.

Exams finally concluded, marking the end of an academic chapter. Sarah, along with our friends, had made plans to meet after the exams, but my eagerness to embrace the next chapter in my personal life led me to dodge those plans. Swiftly, I made my way back home, leaving Sarah wondering about my whereabouts. She sent a curious message, asking where I was, probably scanning the campus for me. However, my attention was solely on preparing for the evening ahead.

Back at home, I allowed myself a moment to relax and unwind. The ambiance was charged with a mix of nervous energy and joyous excitement.

Dad entered the room with a warm smile, inquiring about the recently concluded exams.

"Hey there! How did the exams go?" he asked.

"Oh, hey, Dad! They went well. Feeling a bit relieved now that it's all done," I replied a sense of accomplishment in my voice.

"That's great to hear! You know, you've only got one semester left. Have you thought about what you want to do next?" Dad questioned, his interest piqued.

"Actually, Dad, I've been thinking a lot about it rather than moving to Germany as you wanted. I was considering taking up an internship, especially in content writing and marketing," I shared, bracing myself for his reaction.

"Oh, Content writing and marketing, huh? That sounds interesting. Why an internship, though? You could join the company right away," Dad suggested, genuinely curious.

"Well, Dad, I want to take things one step at a time. I was hoping to intern first, gain some practical experience, and then maybe consider a more permanent role after graduation," I explained, trying to convey my thought process.

"I see. You're already planning for the future. I'm impressed! Why don't you join the company directly, though? You know you're always welcome," Dad said, acknowledging my foresight.

"Absolutely, Dad, and I appreciate that. I just want to make sure I'm well-prepared and have a solid foundation.

Besides, starting with an internship feels like the right way to ease into it, you know?" I reasoned, hoping he'd understand my perspective.

"You're right. It's refreshing to see you take small steps and work your way up. Your internship will be a great opportunity to learn and grow," Dad acknowledged, showing support for my decision.

"Thanks, Dad! I want to make the most of this opportunity, and I believe starting with an internship will allow me to understand the ropes before diving in completely," I expressed, grateful for his understanding.

"I'm proud of you for being proactive about your future. Whenever you're ready, we can discuss the details. I'm here to support you every step of the way," Dad assured, his pride evident in his words.

"Thanks, Dad. I appreciate your support. I'm looking forward to it, but let's focus on acing that last semester first!" I grinned, appreciating the encouragement.

"Absolutely! One step at a time. You've got this!" Dad affirmed.

As we share a smile, my dad adds with a hint of nostalgia, "Your mom would be too proud of you, sweetie. She always believed you'd do great things. You're making her spirit shine with every step you take. I hugged my dad for a while as he left the room.

[Later in the Afternoon]

Vedh: Hey! How did the last exam go?😁

Me: Hey! It went surprisingly well. Feeling a mix of relief and exhaustion. Ready for that evening coffee?😋

Vedh: Absolutely! I'll be waiting for you at the coffee spot. Can't wait to celebrate the end of exams with you. 😊

Me: I'm looking forward to it too, Vedh. Gotta admit, though, I'm a little nervous. Meeting you for the first time, it feels like the butterflies in my stomach are throwing a party. 🦋

Vedh: Nervous, huh? Don't worry; it's just two people sharing a cup of coffee. It's no big deal. But I must confess, the thought of meeting you has me feeling excitement and anticipation.

Me: You always know how to make me feel at ease. I guess it's the unknown that's making me jittery. But hey, a little excitement can be a good thing, right? 😊

Vedh: Absolutely, my dear. Embrace the excitement, let those butterflies dance, and we'll make tonight a memory to cherish. See you soon! ☕💫

Tonight was the night I would finally meet Vedh in person, and the thrill of the unknown added a layer of excitement to the air. I got ready, choosing an outfit that struck the perfect balance between casual and chic.

As the minutes ticked away, I couldn't help but reflect on the twists and turns that had brought me to this moment.

The exams, the calculated evasion of post-exam plans, and the build-up to this evening had created a tapestry of experiences. I felt a mixture of emotions—nervousness, excitement, and a touch of romance.

Chapter 4

A Serendipitous Encounter

I stepped into the cafe, my heart fluttering with excitement. I glanced around, searching for Vedh. My eyes landed on a timid figure tucked away in a corner, and a smile danced across my lips.

Vedh was dressed in a simple polo t-shirt and a pair of black trousers and seemed a little nervous. I noticed that he was shy. He fidgeted his finger, glancing up occasionally, hoping to catch a glimpse of mine. When our eyes finally met, a wave of relief moved over Vedh.

With a graceful stride, I approached Vedh's table. I couldn't help but find his shy demeanor endearing. I did make it a point to observe him closely. I must admit I was amused by his effort to be a gentleman. He rose from his seat, pulling the chair out for me with a charming smile.

"Thank you," I said, taking my seat and feeling a warm glow in my heart. His nervousness only seemed to make me feel more at ease.

I said, "Nice to meet you, Vedh," and smiled.

"Hello, Aaditi," says Vedh, agitated. "If I come out as a little shy, I apologize. Talking to people is not my strongest suit".

"But our chat conversation seems different," I replied, teasing him

As we settled into our seats, the coffee's rich aroma adding to the ambiance, Vedh and I began weaving a more intimate conversation.

"So, Vedh," I said with a playful glint in my eye, "if you were a flavor of coffee, what would you be?"

He grinned, clearly enjoying the question. "Hmm, probably something sweet with a hint of mystery. Like a caramel macchiato. How about you?"

"I'd be a mocha," I replied with a wink. "Sweet, with a bit of a kick. You know, the perfect mix."

Vedh chuckled, "Sounds like a delightful blend. Speaking of delightful, there's something about your smile that's contagious."

Blushing, I teased, "Flattery will get you everywhere, Vedh. Btw, what's your idea of a perfect date?"

He leaned in, his eyes sparkling, "I'd say a night under the stars, with good music, laughter, and, of course, great company."

"That sounds dreamy," I sighed, feeling a tinge of excitement. "Maybe we should plan something like that sometime."

He raised his eyebrows, "Are you asking me out, Aaditi?"

I laughed, "Maybe I am. What do you say?"

He grinned, "I say it's a date. Now, back to our coffee adventure. If our love story were a coffee blend, what would it be called?"

"Definitely 'Eternal Espresso,'" I suggested, "a mix of boldness, sweetness, and a touch of magic."

He nodded, "I like that. A coffee as unique as our story."

Well, indeed. Though I must admit I couldn't resist the temptation of a decent cup of coffee, and that's why I summoned you here—I love this place. By the way, what is your domain of work?

I have founded my own business. My dad has several businesses, but I decided to start something on my own. Thus, we are in the software industry, he said smoothly.

That sounds fascinating! I initially thought of you as an adventurous traveler or travel blogger. I personally love eating a variety of foods. My dream is to start a travel blogger one day. It would be a ton of fun.

With a thoughtful gaze, Vedh asked, "Tell me more about your family, Aaditi. What are they like?"

Smiling, I opened up about my family, "You know, Vedh," I began with a soft smile, "I grew up as a daddy's girl. My mom passed away when I was young, and my dad became my anchor. He's the most protective person I know."

Vedh, sensing the depth of emotion in my words, responded with genuine empathy, "I can't imagine how tough that must have been. Your dad sounds like an amazing person."

I nodded, my eyes reflecting a mixture of nostalgia and love. "He is. Despite the challenges, he raised me to be strong and independent. And, well, a bit overprotective."

His expression softened, and he reached across the table, placing a comforting hand on my hand. "Aaditi, you're incredibly strong, and I can see how much your dad means to you. If there's ever anything you need or anyone you need protection from, I'm here for you."

I was touched by his sincerity and felt a warmth enveloping me. A genuine smile graced my face as I replied, "Thank you, Vedh. That means a lot to me."

We both talked about our individual journeys over the years, including the successes and challenges we had encountered. We discussed our interests and likes. I told him I was an avid reader. He admitted to me that he loved watching films as well. I was astounded by his poise and deft handling of a series of questions. As we talked more, Vedh and I found areas of interest in common and gradually grew closer. His introverted personality grew less of a barrier over time. We both started to find comfort in each other's company.

As we settled into conversation, my anxiety melted away (gradually). My easy-going nature and genuine interest in his thoughts put him at ease. He laughed at my jokes, his laughter like a sweet, unsung melody, enchanting me further.

The hours slipped by unnoticed as we delved into memories; I found myself captivated by Vedh's composure, my eyes sparkling with every word. His presence felt like a soothing balm to my soul, and I found comfort in his company.

Meet Vedh Pathak – a blend of charm, good looks, and a hint of nerdy coolness. Picture a guy who's not just into gaming but also the proud owner of an IT startup. That's Vedh for you! His family, oh, they're into the organic farming game. Sister, parents – the whole shebang. Fields, fresh air, and sustainability vibes all around. But Vedh 's got dreams that stretch beyond the farm fence.

In the day, he's all about green fields and eco-friendly living. When the sun sets, he transforms into this tech-savvy entrepreneur. His startup in IT services is like his baby – born out of a mix of ambition, curiosity, and maybe a bit of late-night gaming inspiration.

His life is a colorful canvas, painted with the contrast of organic roots and tech innovation. It's not just about coding for him; it's about weaving a story that connects tradition with the digital future. Imagine a charming guy with a knack for pixels and a heart for the environment – that's Vedh, making his mark in the world, one line of code at a time.

After our delightful coffee date, We decided to go for an easy walk around. The skies above were cloudy, but we paid no mind to the impending rain. He had forgotten to bring an umbrella. Well, I did bring one myself.

As we strolled along, enjoying each other's company, the first few raindrops began to fall. I wasn't prepared for the rain. His cheeks turned a faint shade of pink as he realized his forgetfulness. I smiled at him, assuring him it was no trouble at all.

We were holding hands as we continued walking. The pitter-patter of raindrops provided a soothing soundtrack to our serendipitous encounter. Vedh's nerves began to resurface as I groped his hand tightly.

Our bodies did occasionally collide as we managed through the overcrowded streets. I could feel Vedh's heart skip a beat at every accidental touch, but I stayed cool. In a moment of courage, He gently wrapped his arm around my shoulder, drawing me closer under the umbrella. His touch was tender, almost as if he feared I might disappear. I leaned into the embrace, feeling the warmth of Vedh's closeness and understanding his gentle nature.

As we continued strolling through the rain-kissed streets, both of us lost ourselves in the comfortable silence that had engulfed us. The umbrella became a symbol of our budding connection, offering shelter not only from the rain but also from the uncertainties and doubts that once plagued our hearts (I could feel it). The gentle embrace of his arm around my shoulder. His small gestures spoke volumes, forging a deeper connection between our souls.

'Would you come with me in my car?' He asked me.

'Sure, but do you mind if I inform my driver, dada, to follow us as he might be waiting for me, I replied.

He nodded, smiling.

I hopped into his car, not bothering to ask him about his plans. The growing trust between us spoke louder than words. As we set out for a long drive, the rain gradually subsided, unveiling a fresh, glistening world by the time we reached our destination. We exchanged a lingering gaze, our hearts entwined in the dance of the shared experience, the journey amplified by the turns we took and the music that echoed our emotions.

After He dropped me near my building, the both of us lingered for a moment, enjoying the closeness we had shared throughout the evening. As we reached the entrance, to our surprise, my cousin was waiting at the gate near my car. Realizing it was best for Vedh to leave, we bid each other a reluctant goodbye.

Once he left, he couldn't help but think about the missed opportunity for an embrace. Wanting to express his feelings, He sent me a message.

Vedh: "Damn, I wanted to hug you, but I had no idea your sister would be there."😘

My phone chimed with Vedh's message, and I couldn't help but smile. I quickly typed a reply, my heart full of longing.

Me: "Then come back and hug me."😁

Vedh: "Should I come back, really?"😀

Me: "No, I'm just kidding. Go home safely, It's pretty late."😇

He felt a mixture of relief and disappointment. He respected my concern for his well-being but yearned for the closeness we had shared.

Me: "Vedh, I think I like you."

Vedh: "Trust me, babe, I like you too. More than words can express."

My face lit up with a radiant smile as I read his messages. I felt a deep connection forming, one that had the potential to grow into something beautiful and profound.

Vedh: "You know, I can't help but admire your nature and how effortlessly you carry yourself. Your confidence and grace are truly captivating. You're not just beautiful on the outside, Aaditi. I love how you talk about your passions and dreams. It's refreshing."

I blushed, feeling a surge of happiness at Vedh's words.

Me: "Thank you. Your shy and gentle nature is what drew me to you in the first place. It's great to be around someone who's so genuine and caring. Your charm isn't just about compliments; it's in the way you make me feel comfortable and appreciated.

Vedh: "I've felt so comfortable around you. From the moment we connected, it felt like I had found a missing piece of myself. Being with you feels like home."

I smiled, feeling a deep sense of contentment.

Me: "That's exactly how I feel, too. Your presence puts me at ease, and I find peace in our moments together. It's as if we're two puzzle pieces that fit perfectly."🖤

Vedh: "Yes, it's like we were meant to find each other again. I cherish the way we can be ourselves around each other, without any pretenses or masks."😁

Me: "Absolutely. It's rare to find someone who accepts you completely, flaws and all. I'm grateful that we can be vulnerable and authentic with each other."😊

Vedh: "Aaditi. Our connection feels like a gift, and I can't wait to explore the depths of our bond."😘

Me: "I feel the same way. This newfound love we share is a treasure, and I'm excited to see where it leads us. "😇

As the night grew deeper, We bid each other goodnight, our hearts filled with excitement for the days ahead.

Vedh: "Goodnight, my sweet Aaditi. I'll dream of the beautiful moments we've shared today."😗😚

Me: "Goodnight. May our dreams intertwine and guide us to a future filled with love and happiness. Until we meet again."
😘

With a heart brimming with affection, I drifted off to sleep.

Rising with the dawn, I laced up my running shoes, determined to squeeze in a refreshing jog before the day began.

As I hit the pavement, the crisp morning air invigorated me, and I couldn't help but feel a surge of energy. In the midst of my run, I decided to ping Sarah, suggesting a quick breakfast catch-up before our college day kicked off.

To my surprise, Sarah's response was still pending, leaving the plans hanging in the balance. Undeterred, I continued my jog, hoping for a positive reply later. As I cooled down and checked my phone, Vedh's message popped up. He shared that he was on a work trip in Mumbai, and he had a lovely time the previous evening. However, he mentioned that he would be flying off early in the afternoon, making him unavailable for the rest of the day.

While a bit disappointed about the unconfirmed breakfast plans with Sarah, Vedh's message brought a mix of emotions—gratefulness for his update and a sweet note about the time we had shared the previous evening. With the sun rising higher, I decided to embrace the unexpected turn of events and look forward to the day's unfolding surprises.

I couldn't contain my excitement after the wonderful date I had with him. As I was returning home from college, a constant stream of thoughts about our time together flooded my mind. I was eager to share the details with Sarah.

I dialed Sarah's number, my fingers tingling. But to my disappointment, Sarah's phone went unanswered. Undeterred, I decided to send her a flurry of text messages.

Me: "Hey, Sarah! I had the most incredible coffee date yesterday. I can't wait to tell you all about it!"😏

Hours later, with no response, my excitement grew even more, making me increasingly impatient.

Me: "Sarah, pick up your phone! I need to talk to you. It's urgent!"😑

Sarah, busy with her own affairs, finally noticed the barrage of missed calls and messages from me. Intrigued by my urgency, she quickly called me.

Sarah: "Hey, Aaditi! Sorry for not answering earlier. I was at a wedding, and before I answered your call, my battery had drained! What's going on? You seem really excited!"

My voice bubbled with enthusiasm as I recounted the details of my coffee date with Vedh. I gushed about his shy nature, his genuine behavior, and the strong connection we felt.

Me: "Sarah, you won't believe how amazing it was. Vedh is like no one I've ever met. He's kind and attentive, and there's this undeniable chemistry between us."

On the other end of the call, I could sense Sarah's smile, her happiness for me shining through.

Sarah: "That sounds incredible, Aaditi. I'm thrilled you had a great time. But, you know, take things slow and be cautious. After what happened with Aarav, I don't want to see you get hurt again."

Me: "I get it, Sarah. I've learned from my past mistakes, and I won't rush into anything. But this feels different, you know? Vedh is so genuine, and I can't help but be excited about the possibilities."

Sarah: "I trust your judgment. Just remember to listen to your heart and instincts. I want to see you happy, and if Vedh is the one who brings you that happiness, then I'll support you all the way."

Me: "Thanks, Sarah. Your friendship means the world to me. I'll take things slow, and I promise to keep you updated on how things progress with Vedh. I'm just grateful to have found someone who makes me feel this way."

Sarah: "I'm glad, Aaditi. You deserve all the happiness in the world. I can't wait to hear more about Vedh and see where this journey takes you. Just remember, I'm here for you, no matter what."

With our conversation coming to an end, Later at night, I got a message from Vedh.

Vedh: Hey babe, are you awake?😊

I replied, "Yes, sorta. What's up?"😇

Vedh: I couldn't sleep, and I was thinking about you. You've got that effect on me.😍😘

I blushed, "Haha, Compliments like that might just earn you a VIP pass to my good graces. Sweetie. What were you thinking?" 🤪😋

Vedh: Well, that's easy! I just remember our time together today. Can't get those moments out of my head.😍😍

I smiled, "Likewise. It was a great evening."😁

Vedh: You looked stunning, by the way. Couldn't take my eyes off you.😘😘

I teased, "Oh, stop it. You're making me blush through the phone."😁😉

Vedh: It's true, though. And I can't wait for the next time I get to see you.😊

I chuckled, "Well, I might just have to make that happen sooner rather than later."😁

Vedh: I'd love that. Maybe we can plan something special?🙂

I playfully responded, "Hmm, surprises are always welcome. What do you have in mind?"😉

Vedh: You know, I was wondering, why does a guy always have to take the lead when it comes to proposing? What if a girl wants to do it?😬

I pondered for a moment, "That's an interesting thought. Why do you ask?"🤔

Vedh: Just thinking aloud. I mean, if I had to, I'd say yes in a heartbeat.🙄

I couldn't help but smile at his openness, "Well, noted. I'll keep that in mind.😉

And so, the conversation took an intriguing turn, delving into discussions about relationships and traditions, adding a layer of depth to our late-night exchange.

As we prepared for last semester, we looked back on our shared adventures with fondness and gratitude. Our college days had been more than just lectures and exams; they had been a whirlwind of discovery and friendship. We learned that sometimes, the best adventures are the ones you create with the people who share your enthusiasm for life.

I sat beside Sarah, a fellow adventurer with a perpetual sparkle in her eyes. But today, even her enthusiasm seemed to wane. Then, Rudhay, the mischievous rebel who sat on the other side of Sarah, leaned over and whispered something that changed the course of the day.

"Sarah," he whispered, "I've got an idea."

Sarah's eyes lit up immediately, and I leaned closer, intrigued. I had always admired her sense of spontaneity. "Tell me, Rudhay," she urged.

He grinned, his voice barely a whisper. "Let's ditch college today and go on an adventure."

Sarah's excitement was palpable. "Where to?" she asked.

Without hesitation, He replied, "How about Jaipur?"

The idea was daring, reckless even, but it was irresistible. Sarah and Rudhay quietly slipped out of the lecture hall, leaving behind our bewildered classmates. Soon, they gathered the rest of us—Monish, Hemakshi, and me. Friends who, like Sarah and Rudhay, craved adventure. They explained their audacious plan, and to our surprise, we needed a little convincing. In mere minutes, the group was assembled and ready to embark on a spontaneous adventure.

"Are you serious?" Monish said as we made our way to the cafeteria.

"Well, yes." Rudhay and Hemakshi answered in tandem. I kept staring at him as he said this.

"But we don't have any luggage," said Sarah.

We'll buy a few clothes when we reach Jaipur, he said.

In a whimsical moment, we surrendered to spontaneity, sharing playful glances that sparked the decision to ditch lectures in favor of embracing adventure. The alluring combination of Jaipur's lively streets, historical allure, and the promise of delectable local cuisine proved too tempting to resist. We set out on a culinary escapade, ready to savor the flavors of Jaipur, making our day of exploration a delightful journey through both the city's history and its rich, aromatic delicacy offerings.

Chapter 5
The Jaipur Escapade

We ditched our drivers. As the wheels of Rudhay's car left the city behind, we left behind the monotony of college and embraced the open road that led us to Jaipur. The journey was filled with laughter, music, and an inexplicable sense of freedom. College felt like a distant memory, and the road to Jaipur promised a thrilling escapade.

As we set out on our road trip from Delhi to Jaipur, I couldn't help but feel a surge of excitement. The early morning sun cast a warm, golden glow over the bustling streets of Delhi as I navigated through the city's chaotic traffic. My adventure was about to begin, and I was eager to explore the vibrant culture and rich history of Rajasthan.

Leaving the urban sprawl behind, we merged onto the open highway. The road stretched out before me, a ribbon of asphalt cutting through the picturesque countryside. Fields of golden wheat swayed in the breeze, and quaint villages dotted the landscape. The gentle hum of the car's engine was accompanied by our favorite road trip playlist, setting the perfect soundtrack for the journey ahead.

After about a few hours or so, I could see that Rudhay needed some time to recuperate. We decided to take it easy for the afternoon, allowing him to rest and regain his energy, and I took over the wheels.

As I drove further, the landscape began to gradually transform. I crossed the state border into Rajasthan, and the arid plains of the region came into view. The bright colors of Rajasthan's traditional attire, the turbans and saris, seemed to blend seamlessly with the earthy tones of the desert. While I was driving, I noticed that my phone battery had unexpectedly drained, leaving me unable to inform Vedh about a spontaneous road trip plan with my friends. "I hope he isn't too concerned about me," I pondered silently.

One of the highlights of our road trip was our planned stop at the Neemrana Fort Palace, a magnificent heritage hotel. As I pulled into the grand entrance, the sight of the fort took my breath away. Its imposing structure stood like a sentinel from an ancient era, a witness to the rich history of Rajasthan.

I parked our car and made our way inside the fort. The cool, shadowy corridors seemed to whisper stories of centuries past. The walls were adorned with ancient paintings and intricate carvings that spoke of the fort's regal history. I couldn't resist exploring every nook and cranny, climbing ancient staircases, and discovering hidden chambers. We reached the highest point, the world seemed to stretch out before me in all its glory. The wind gently tousled my hair, and I couldn't help but feel like I was on top of the world. We clicked pictures and moved further to our hotel, a beautiful heritage property radiating the regal essence of the region. After a quick freshening up and plugging in my phone, I noticed there was no network in the room, probably because we were on the outskirts. With the evening at my disposal, We decided to embark on my first adventure in Jaipur, a visit to the majestic Amber Fort. One of the most captivating parts of the Amber Fort was the Sheesh Mahal or Hall of Mirrors. It was a chamber entirely covered in tiny, glistening mirrors that reflected even the faintest glimmer of light. Stepping into this ethereal space felt like entering a fairy tale.

As the day began to wane, we descended from the fort and made our way to the bustling bazaars of Jaipur. The markets were a sensory overload, with vibrant textiles, intricate jewelry, and aromatic street food stalls at every turn. I couldn't resist the temptation to shop for souvenirs.

Despite my attempts to charge my phone, it hadn't reached full battery yet. After the network was eventually restored, I was greeted with a flurry of messages from Vedh, filled with concern and worry. "Hey beautiful, good morning! Are you busy?" "Hey, where are you? I tried reaching out!" "You are scaring me. Can you call, please?" Before I could respond to his messages, my phone began to ring, displaying Vedh's name on the screen. I moved aside from my group and answered.

Vedh's voice echoed with relief through the phone as he exclaimed, "Babe, finally! Where have you been? I've been trying to reach you."

Apologizing, I responded, "Hey, sorry, there was no network in the hotel. I'm in Jaipur."

Concern laced Vedh's next words, "You had me worried. Are you okay? What happened? Why in Jaipur? Is everything okay?"

Assuring him, I said, "I'm fine, Vedh. Just a network glitch. Didn't want you to stress."

Softly, Vedh expressed, "Sweetheart, I was scared something happened to you. Can you please keep me posted?"

Grateful for his concern, I replied, "I appreciate your concern, baby. I'm safe and sound, I promise. You won't believe what happened. Rudhay and Sarah's group decided to ditch lectures and take a road trip to Jaipur. It was sudden, and we left in a hurry. Sorry, my phone battery was drained, and there were network issues around here."

Vedh, in a gentle tone, remarked, "You could drop a message, babe. However, it's good to hear your voice. I missed you. When are you heading back?"

Smiling, I confessed, "Missed you too. Tomorrow morning! Once I'm back, we can catch up."

"Sure thing! But please, if possible, keep me posted," Vedh requested.

"Of course, baby, I will!" I assured him.

"Take care of yourself and your friends. Can't wait to talk again. Love you," He said with warmth.

Surprised by the sudden declaration, I teased, "Love me?"

He chuckled, "Too soon?"

"Hmmm," I replied playfully.

"See you," He said, wrapping up the call.

I hung up the call, and as his tender words, "I love you," hung in the air, a warm blush crept across my cheeks, painting a canvas of emotions. The weight of those three words carried a sweetness that resonated within me, causing my heart to flutter with joy. At that moment, the world seemed to pause, and a soft, radiant glow enveloped us. I was grateful for the profound simplicity of love's expression. I joined my friends back. The evening brought a different kind of magic to Jaipur. The city's iconic monuments, including the Hawa Mahal and the City Palace, were beautifully illuminated, casting a warm, golden glow over the Pink City.

For dinner, We decided to savor the flavors of Rajasthan with a traditional Rajasthani meal. We found a charming local restaurant known for its authentic cuisine. The meal included dal baati churma, a Rajasthani specialty that combines savory lentils, baked wheat balls, and sweet crumbled wheat. The explosion of flavors on my taste buds was a true culinary delight, and we savored every bite.

As we settled into our hotel room that night, I couldn't help but reflect on the day's journey. The road trip from Delhi to Jaipur was a mesmerizing adventure through changing landscapes and rich cultural experiences.

We made ourselves comfortable on the beds, surrounded by the heritage walls that held stories of times gone by. Sarah, with a mischievous glint in her eyes, nudged me and asked, "So, spill the details about Vedh. How was your date?"

A smile crept onto my face as I began to narrate the evening. "You know, it was like a dream, Sarah. He made every moment special, from the way he looked at me to the way he laughed at my silly jokes. We talked about everything, and I could feel this connection like we've known each other forever."

Sarah, listening intently, chimed in, "That sounds amazing! What did you guys do?"

"We started with a quaint cafe, then took a stroll in the park, and then he dropped me home. The simplicity of it all made it so magical," I shared, my voice carrying the warmth of the memories.

She grinned, "I can feel the butterflies just hearing about it. Did he say anything special?"

A blush colored my cheeks as I continued, "He complimented my smile, and when he said he enjoyed every moment with me, I felt this: I don't know, spark? It was like we created our own little universe for those few hours."

Sarah, with a knowing smile, replied, "Sounds like you found something special, my friend."

Encouragement and warmth filled the room as Sarah spoke, "You know what, Aaditi? I'm happy for you. You deserve all the happiness in the world. Just make sure he treats you right."

Gratefully, I responded, "Thank you, Sarah. Your support means a lot to me. Vedh has been nothing but kind and genuine so far. I feel comfortable around him."

From behind the door, Rudhay, who had been silently listening to our conversation, added his voice with a hint of concern, "Aaditi, while it's great to see you happy, just make sure you're not rushing into anything. Remember what happened with Aarav? We don't want history repeating itself."

Nodding, I acknowledged Rudhay's words of caution, "I appreciate your concern, Rudhay. Trust me, I'm being cautious. I've learned from my past experiences, and I won't let my guard down easily. But for now, Vedh makes me feel special, and I want to explore where this connection takes us."

Rudhay, reassured by my response, added, "As long as you're aware and taking it slow, I'm here to support you, Aaditi. Just don't forget to prioritize your own happiness and well-being."

"Today was incredible, guys. Thank you, Sarah and Rudhay, for being here for me and helping me overcome that intrusion. I'm so lucky to have you all," I expressed, feeling grateful for the support of my friends.

Sarah chimed in, "We're always here for you, Aaditi. You deserve happiness, and we won't let anyone take that away from you."

Determined, I asserted, "I'm ready to leave the past behind and embrace the future. Vedh makes me happy, and I won't let anything or anyone ruin that."

Before I dozed off, I took a moment to share the highlights of my day with Vedh. Excitement filled me as I sent him pictures of my friends and me, capturing our laughter and the picturesque view of the city of Jaipur.

Me: Hey, sorry, I was pretty much disconnected the whole day. Your concern when you called really touched my heart!

Vedh: No need to apologize, Aaditi. I was worried. You know, I really care about you. It's strange; it feels like you're my responsibility now.

Me: Aww, Vedh, look at these pictures! We had so much fun in Jaipur today. Wish you were here with us.

Vedh: Wow! The pictures look amazing. I can almost feel the joy through them. I wish I could have been there too.

Me: I missed you throughout the day. It's incredible how easily I feel close to you.

Vedh: I missed you too. It warms my heart to know that you felt connected to me even when we were apart. Your friends seem awesome.

Me, They are! We had a fantastic time together. It made me realize how lucky I am to have such wonderful friends and someone as special as you in my life.

Vedh: I feel the same way, Aaditi.

Our messages continued to flow, filled with sweet words. My heart fluttered as I read heartfelt words. The distance between us seemed to fade away, replaced by the growing affection and emotional closeness we shared.

The calm of the night shattered, and a strange feeling woke me up suddenly. My heart was pounding, and I felt a chill. It seemed like someone was lingering outside my hotel room, a presence making the night uneasy.

I lay there, breathing fast, trying to figure out if it was just my imagination. Were those footsteps or a whisper? I couldn't tell in the silent darkness. Something didn't feel right.

I decided to wake up Sarah, hoping her presence would calm me down. I spoke to her in a shaky voice, sharing my uneasy feelings. We checked the hallway, but there was no sign of anyone. It was like the mysterious presence had vanished, leaving us with unanswered questions.

Back in our room, the strange incident lingered, making it hard to forget. Despite Sarah being there, the night's events kept bothering me. Sleep eluded me as I tried to make sense of the mystery that disrupted the peace in Jaipur.

The morning sun greeted us as we ventured into Kishanpole bazaar for a day of shopping. However, a disconcerting feeling surfaced once more—a sense that someone was discreetly tracking our steps. It wasn't the market that excited me, but the unsettling notion of being watched.

I leaned in toward Rudhay and softly expressed my concerns. "I have a feeling someone's following us again."

Rudhay's eyes darted around, assessing the bustling crowd. "Are you sure?" he asked, a tinge of concern evident in his voice.

I nodded, feeling a shiver down my spine. "Just like yesterday, I can't shake off this sensation. Someone's definitely trailing us."

Sarah joined in, composed yet cautious. "Let's not jump to conclusions, but we should stay vigilant."

Despite attempting to blend in with the crowd, the feeling of being observed persisted. Then, my gaze caught an unknown group of men in a hooded cloak, shadowing us from a distance, their identity concealed. A sense of unease washed over me.

"We need to take action," I urged, urgency coloring my voice.

Rudhay agreed, his protective instincts kicking in. "Let's change our route and head toward a busier area. Maybe we can lose them."

We navigated through the lively market, aiming for a more crowded section, hoping to shake off our mysterious followers. However, to my dismay, the figure persisted, adeptly navigating the crowd to stay on our trail.

"It's not a coincidence. They're purposefully tailing us," I whispered, my heart pounding with apprehension.

Sarah swiftly formulated a plan. "Let's find someone we trust, a security guard or a shopkeeper who might be of help."

Quickly, we approached a nearby shop and explained our concerns to the shopkeeper, who promptly summoned a security guard. With their discreet assistance, we managed to slip away from the market, seeking refuge in a nearby cafe, our senses heightened for any sign of our shadow.

Jaipur's beauty was juxtaposed with my constant wariness, suspecting that Aarav might have extended his reach to this bustling city. The thought that his influence might stretch so far, orchestrating disturbances from a distance, unnerved me deeply.

"Aaditi, I understand you're feeling uneasy, but I think you might be overthinking this," Rudhay said, his voice calm and reassuring.

His words, though soothing, didn't immediately dispel the knots of worry in my mind. "Rudhay, I can't help but feel like something's off. It's not just a passing thought; it's like a constant presence, a feeling of being watched," I replied, trying to convey the gravity of my concerns.

"I get it, and your feelings are valid," Rudhay acknowledged, gently placing a hand on my shoulder. "But sometimes our minds tend to play tricks on us, especially when we're stressed or anxious. Aarav being in your thoughts might be making you hyper-aware of everything around you."

His attempt to rationalize the situation offered a flicker of comfort, yet the unsettling feeling persisted. "But what if I'm not imagining it? What if Aarav's really involved in all this?" I countered, a trace of worry still evident in my voice.

Rudhay maintained his composure, offering a reassuring smile. "We'll take precautions, but let's not let this overshadow our time here in Jaipur. Remember, we're here to enjoy and experience this beautiful city. Trust me, everything will be okay."

His words carried a sense of conviction, a promise of safety that I desperately needed. I nodded, trying to heed his advice and push the apprehensions aside, willing myself to embrace the essence of Jaipur without letting fear cloud my experiences.

Amidst the busy street vendors and enticing aromas, they encouraged me to explore the local delicacies. Rudhay handed me a plate filled with an array of delights, including the aromatic fragrance of dal baati churma, the rich allure of laal maas, and the savory appeal of gatte ki sabzi.

Sarah, ever watchful, assured me, “We’re here for you, Aaditi. Let’s relish these flavors and soak in Jaipur’s charm.”

Savoring bites of kachori, the spicy thrill of mirchi bada, and the sumptuousness of Rajasthani thali, I found myself gradually letting go. Surrounded by laughter and the rich tapestry of Jaipur’s culinary treasures, the worries that had clouded my thoughts began to fade into the background.

As they made their way back, Sarah suggested a spontaneous stop at Jal Mahal. “Hey, why don’t we take a quick break at Jal Mahal? It’s such a peaceful spot,” she proposed, steering their path toward the iconic palace situated amidst the serene Man Sagar Lake.

Exiting the vehicle, the serene atmosphere embraced us, the gentle breeze carrying a sense of serenity across the shimmering water. The beauty of the palace reflected against the stillness of the lake presented a picture of calmness. Surrounded by the quiet beauty of Jal Mahal and the peaceful vista, a sense of calmness enveloped me. The concerns that had occupied my thoughts seemed to dissipate in the tranquil ambiance of this serene setting.

Observing the change in my demeanor, Sarah smiled warmly. "Feels peaceful, right?" she remarked softly.

Nodding in agreement, letting the serene ambiance of Jal Mahal wash away the remnants of unease, allowing myself to immerse in the peacefulness that surrounded us.

As we stepped back into our everyday lives, we knew that Jaipur had changed us. We were no longer just students attending lectures and studying for exams. We were adventurers, seekers of spontaneity, and friends who had shared a journey that would forever be etched in our hearts.

After returning home, I enjoyed a quiet dinner with my dad. As we shared a meal, our conversation briefly touched upon my trip to Jaipur. He smiled warmly and remarked, "It's good to see you having fun with your friends. These moments matter, Aaditi. Cherish them." In those simple words, I felt the warmth of his support and understanding, grateful for his trust in me.

In the soft glow of the video call, Vedh's face lit up as he greeted me, "Hey there! How was your day?"

"It was good, but I'm pretty tired. The day was quite eventful," I replied, exhaustion evident in my voice.

Vedh, ever the charmer, couldn't resist a teasing smirk, "Tired, huh? Well, tired looks cute on you."

Laughing, I playfully protested, "Aw, please stop it."

Grinning mischievously, Vedh persisted, "But you are cute, even when tired. I miss you, you know?"

Smiling warmly, I admitted, "I miss you too. It's been a long day."

In a playful tone, Vedh added, "I wish I could be there to give you a goodnight kiss on those cute cheeks."

Blushing, I responded, "Vedh! You and your cheesy lines."

Laughing heartily, Vedh confessed, "Can't help it. You make me all gushy and romantic."

Changing the subject, I hinted at a surprise, "Well, I have something to share. I've got a surprise plan for us."

Curious, Vedh asked, "Surprise? What is it?"

With a mischievous glint in my eye, I teased, "Ah, that's a secret for now. But get ready to be astonished."

Excitement filled Vedh's voice, "Now, you've piqued my curiosity. When do I get to know?"

Teasingly, I replied, "Patience, my dear Vedh. All in good time. It's going to be fun!"

Enthusiastically, Vedh declared, "I can't wait."

Our conversation concluded with the promise of something exciting to come, leaving a sense of anticipation hanging in the air. As we exchanged goodnights, happy thoughts and eager anticipation filled our hearts.

Chapter 6
Love is All We Got

(2 Months later)

Since wrapping up my final exams, I've been holding back my feelings, opting to avoid meeting Vedh. I wanted to give my undivided attention to the last stretch of my studies. Now that it's all done, I'm ready to open up and share what's been on my mind.

My emotions swirled like a tempest within me. Vedh was someone who had slowly become an integral part of my life. We shared countless moments of laughter, support, and understanding. Our connection had grown stronger with each passing day, and I cherished the bond we had formed.

But this thought of a proposal... It was unexpected, catching me off guard. My mind raced with a flood of thoughts and questions. Was I ready for this level of commitment? Did I truly see a future with Vedh? Was he the one who would stand by my side through thick and thin?

I closed my eyes, seeking soothe in the silence of my thoughts. Flashes of our memories danced through my mind, reminding me of the happiness we had shared. The tender moments, the inside jokes, and the countless conversations that had deepened our connection.

Yet, alongside those joyful memories, doubts whispered their way into my consciousness. What about our differences? Would they create obstacles in the long run? What about my dreams and aspirations? Would they be compromised or overshadowed?

But in the depths of my contemplation, one truth remained constant—I couldn't ignore the significance of Vedh in my life. The way he made me feel seen, understood, and valued. The way his smile could melt away my worries, and his touch could calm the storms within me. His presence had become an anchor, grounding me in moments of chaos.

And so, after days of introspection and countless conversations with Vedh. I found myself slowly coming to a realization. Love was not a flawless equation, nor was it devoid of challenges. It was a choice - a choice to embrace vulnerability, to grow together, and to weather the storms that life would inevitably throw our way.

"Hey Vedh," I messaged, a blend of excitement and vulnerability in my words, "what do you say we take this beyond the screens? Two months of our virtual dance, and I'm craving the warmth of a face-to-face. Are you up for it?"

Vedh's response was swift, a surge of heartfelt enthusiasm, "Aaditi, absolutely! I've been hoping for the same. Any thoughts on where we could make this happen?"

Seizing the moment, I revealed my plan with a touch of romantic flair, "I've got just the place in mind. There's this enchanting restaurant by a pool—the ambiance is pure magic. What do you think?"

Vedh, with a heartwarming simplicity, replied, "Sounds like a dream, Aaditi! I'm all in. Let's make it happen."

On the day of the date, what caught me off guard was Vedh picking me up, and there, in his hands, a burst of color and fragrance – a lovely bouquet of orchids, adding an extra touch of sweetness to the evening. Feeling a mix of excitement and nervousness. As they sat by the poolside, the soft glow of the surrounding lights created a romantic atmosphere.

As I expressed my delight, Vedh, ever the gentleman, responded, "Your presence makes everything more magical. You look absolutely stunning tonight."

His words brought a smile to my face, which widened when he presented me with a beautiful bouquet of orchids. I couldn't help but inquire about the inspiration behind such a romantic gesture.

"Well," Vedh began, "I wanted tonight to be as special as possible. You deserve all the beauty and joy in the world."

His sincerity touched my heart, and I couldn't help but express my gratitude. "You're already making it unforgettable. I appreciate the effort you've put into this."

With a warm smile, Vedh raised his glass and said, "Anything for you. Here's to more moments like these and to us."

"To us," I echoed, clinking glasses in a silent toast to the beauty of the evening and the promise of more shared moments ahead.

Our conversation flowed effortlessly, filled with laughter and shared dreams. The evening felt like a fairytale as if time had slowed down just for us. As our dinner came to an end, I suggested taking a walk near the nearby lake, a serene spot known for its beauty.

"Vedh, let's take a walk near the lake," I said, my voice filled with excitement. "The moonlight reflecting on the water creates a mesmerizing view.

His eyes lit up. "Aaditi, I couldn't think of a more perfect way to end our date. Walking by your side, hand in hand, and witnessing the beauty of nature... It's a dream I never want to wake up from."

We strolled along the path, our fingers intertwined, feeling a deep sense of connection. The world around us seemed to fade away as we got lost in each other's company. As we reached a bench overlooking the lake, we sat down, silently admiring the serene scene.

The moon cast a gentle glow on the water, and the night was filled with the soft sounds of nature. But then, as if nature itself wanted to add a touch of magic to our evening, the sky suddenly darkened, and raindrops started to fall gently from above. We looked at each other, our eyes filled with excitement and a hint of mischief. The unexpected rain only made our night together more unforgettable. In the quiet ambiance of the evening, with a hint of nervousness, I finally mustered the courage to express what had been lingering in my heart.

"(Nervously) Vedh, there's something I need to tell you. I... I love you. Cutting to the chase here – you've become a highlight reel in the story of my life. Swiping through moments, it's clear that you're more than just a right swipe. Let's ditch the filters and make this connection official. Vedh, would you be down for more than just casual chats and join me in creating some real-life moments?

The air seemed to be still for a moment as Vedh took in my words. His response, delivered softly, carried a weight of emotion that resonated deeply.

"Aaditi, your openness, and realness have only deepened my feelings for you. There's something truly special about the connection we share, and I can't deny that I've fallen for you. So, Let's turn these virtual sparks into real-life fireworks! I'm ready to explore where this journey with you takes us because, truth be told, I love you too."

In that tender exchange, the unspoken feelings found a voice, weaving a new chapter in our story. The vulnerability and sincerity of the moment created a connection that bound us together, marking the beginning of a shared journey filled with love and companionship.

My face lit up with joy, and I reached out to hold his hand, intertwining our fingers. The electricity that passed between us confirmed that we were embarking on a beautiful journey together, hand in hand.

"Vedh," I said, smiling, "I'm so happy to hear that. I can't wait to explore this love with you and create countless memories together. Thank you for being in my life."

Our love felt invincible and pure, and the future seemed full of promise and adventure. We continued our walk, hearts intertwined and souls aligned, ready to embrace the beautiful journey that awaited us.

He gently said, "Aaditi, the happiness I feel right now is immeasurable. You've touched my soul in ways I never thought possible. Thank you for choosing me and for loving me. I promise to cherish you and our relationship with all my heart and to protect you."

In that rain-soaked walk, my confession and his reciprocation solidified our bond, creating a foundation of love and trust that would stand the test of time. The intensity of our emotions still hung in the air, and an unspoken desire lingered between us. Sensing the moment, I leaned in closer to him, my eyes filled with longing.

In that instant, as our lips met, it felt like the world around us disappeared. Our kiss was filled with all the passion. It was a moment of pure, unspoken love where our hearts connected in a way that words could never fully express.

The kiss came to an end, and we slowly pulled away, our foreheads touching, our breaths intertwined. Our eyes met, and in that gaze, we saw our future, brimming with love, adventure, and unwavering support.

I whispered, "Woah, that was quite amazing!" He just winked. We held each other close, our hearts still racing from the intensity of the moment. He was prepared to leave; I held onto him, not wanting the night to end. We shared one last tender kiss, savoring the sweetness of our love.

I watched him go, and a feeling of contentment washed over me, knowing that our love had been sealed by the rain and our commitment to each other. The rain had brought us together, and it was a reminder that love could bloom in the most unexpected and beautiful ways.

With a heart full of love, I looked forward to the next chapter of our journey together, knowing that our love would only grow stronger with time. I quickly texted him.

Me: Baby, I can't wait for more moments like this, where our love ignites and sets our hearts ablaze. Until we meet again, know that you'll always be in my thoughts. 😘

Vedh: I am the happiest today. I love you, Aaditi! Take care. Until we meet again. 😍

The next few days felt monumentally significant in the grand scheme of my life. Despite the apparent monotony of daily routines, there was a profound sense of change in the air, a shift in perspective that had been ignited by that magical night with Vedh.

As I went about my daily tasks, there was a burgeoning excitement in my heart, a sense that something extraordinary was on the horizon. I eagerly wait for our next meeting, knowing that each encounter with him will bring new dimensions to our growing relationship.

I had just gone to college to return books for the day and was about to head home when something caught my attention. Standing near the college entrance was Vedh, a mischievous smile playing on his lips. His unexpected presence took me by surprise, and my heart skipped a beat.

The sight of him waiting for me sent a rush of excitement and joy through my veins. It was as if the universe itself had conspired to bring us together once again. I couldn't help but break into a wide smile as I approached him.

"Hey," I exclaimed, my voice filled with both surprise and delight. "What are you doing here?"

He stepped closer, his eyes filled with warmth and affection. "I couldn't wait until our next planned meeting. I wanted to see you now, to spend some time together."

His words filled my heart with happiness. In disbelief, I questioned, "But how did you know I would be coming out now?"

Grinning, He replied, "I have my ways of finding out. I wanted to surprise you and spend some more time together."

I couldn't help but be swept away by his thoughtfulness. I knew he went out of his way to make this surprise happen, and it touched me deeply.

Blushing, I admitted, "You always manage to surprise me, Vedh. I can't believe you're here, right outside my college. What do you have planned?"

Excitedly, He suggested, "Today, you're going to skip your gym and have an adventure of our own. How about we go watch a movie together?"

My eyes widened with surprise. The idea of ditching my usual routine and spending the day with him was incredibly enticing.

Giggling, I responded, “You’re full of surprises! I would love to go on this unplanned adventure with you. Let’s go!”

We hopped onto Vedh’s scooter, and as we zipped through the busy streets, the wind brushed against our faces, filling us with a sense of freedom and excitement. Arriving at the movie theater, we browsed through the various options and settled on a romantic comedy. We purchased our tickets and entered the darkened theater, finding seats in the back row.

As the movie began, I found myself laughing at the comedic moments, and my heart warmed during the tender scenes. Beside me, He stole glances, his eyes sparkling with adoration.

It was a simple yet beautiful date, filled with shared laughter and stolen glances in the dimly lit theater. The movie became a backdrop to our own love story, a reminder of the joy and affection we felt for each other. In those precious hours, it was as if time stood still, and all that mattered was the bond we were building and the happiness we found in each other’s presence.

He leaned in, his voice a soft whisper, “This day feels so special. Just being here with you, away from our usual routine, makes me appreciate every moment even more.”

Whispering back, I shared the sentiment, “I feel the same way. Today feels like an escape from reality, and I’m grateful to be sharing it with you.”

The chemistry that had been building since our first meeting seemed to intensify in the darkened theater.

Lost in the moment and the intimacy of the cinema, Vedh and I found ourselves drawn closer to each other. The surrounding people and noise seemed to fade into the background as our focus became solely on each other.

Our eyes locked, and without saying a word, our hearts communicated a desire that couldn't be contained. In that instant, we leaned in and shared a tender kiss, our emotions and love for each other palpable.

As we embraced each other in the movie theater, we were both aware of the people around us, but our love and passion took precedence. Our connection transcended the physical space, and for that brief moment, it was just the two of us, lost in our own world.

In the hushed tones of a whispered exchange, I confessed, "I feel so connected to you. I've never felt this way before. You make me feel alive."

He reciprocated the sentiment and whispered back, "Being with you feels like a dream. You bring so much joy and happiness into my life. I can't imagine my days without you."

A sudden interruption emerged in the form of Vedh's ringing phone. Apologetically, he glanced at me, his expression reflecting a mix of concern and regret.

"I'm really sorry, Aaditi," He sighed, "but there's an urgent issue at the office that I need to resolve. I hate that it's interrupting our time together."

Understanding the demands of his professional life, I reassured him, "It's okay, Vedh. I understand. Work can be unpredictable."

He suggested an alternative, "Would you mind accompanying me to the office for a while? I promise it won't take long, and I'd really appreciate your company."

Despite the change of plans, I nodded, acknowledging the necessity of the situation. "Of course, . Let's go together. We can make the best of it."

Entering his office was like stepping into controlled chaos. The space was adorned with sleek, modern furniture and large windows that offered a panoramic view of the city lights below. Despite the hurried pace of the office environment, there was an air of efficiency that permeated the room.

Vedh's cabin, tucked away in a corner, provided a brief respite from the buzzing activity outside. The walls were adorned with a few framed photographs capturing moments of joy and achievement. A neatly organized desk held a laptop, a notepad, and a strategically placed stress ball.

As He delved into the urgent matter at hand, he made an effort to ensure my comfort. In a thoughtful gesture, he ordered pizza and coffee, sensing the need for a pleasant distraction amidst the office hustle.

The aroma of freshly brewed coffee wafted through the cabin, mixing with the faint hum of distant office chatter. The pizza arrived, adorned with an array of toppings that hinted at a taste of indulgence in the midst of a busy day.

Taking a moment to unwind, I motioned toward a seating area equipped with a small coffee table and a comfortable chair. On the side, a gaming console caught my eye. It was a PlayStation, a subtle hint at Vedh's means of stress relief during demanding workdays.

Midway through the hustle of addressing urgent office matters, Vedh stepped back into his cabin, only to find me engrossed in a gaming session on his PlayStation. A subtle surprise painted his expression, a mix of amusement and awe.

"Wow, Aaditi! I didn't know you were into gaming," He exclaimed, clearly intrigued by this unexpected side of me.

With a mischievous grin, I handed him a controller, saying, "Care to join in? I might surprise you."

He was, still slightly taken aback, accepted the challenge with a laugh, "Alright then, let's see what you've got."

As the game unfolded on the screen, the friendly competition became a source of laughter. He quickly realized that my gaming skills were not to be underestimated, and the challenge took an interesting turn.

With determination in his eyes, He proposed a bet, "How about this, Baby? If you win, I'll take you to one of your favorite places. But if I win, well, you'll find out soon enough."

The stakes were set, and the game intensified. Laughter echoed in the cabin, turning an impromptu gaming session into a memorable moment.

In the aftermath of the game, His victorious grin persisted as he leaned back in his chair, reveling in the moment. A mischievous glint in his eyes, he broke the post-game silence with a playful suggestion.

"Well, Aaditi, it seems luck was on my side this time," He chuckled, his tone holding a hint of mischief. "I suppose the winner deserves a... closer reward."

His suggestion hung in the air, a tempting invitation. Without missing a beat, He pulled me on his lap, a twinkle in his eye.

I gently extricated myself from the unexpected closeness, a small smile playing on my lips. "Mr Pathak, let's keep it professional here, shall we?" I teased, trying to diffuse the moment with a lighthearted tone.

He grinned, "Aaditi," he began, his voice taking on a more earnest tone, "there's something I've always wanted to confess."

I looked at him, curiosity piqued, as he continued, "I've always had this secret desire to share a moment, perhaps a make out, in the office. Call it a fantasy or a forbidden wish, but the idea has always lingered in the back of my mind."

With a soft smile, I broke the silence, "Well, Vedh, they say there's a first time for everything, isn't it?"

The air crackled with newfound energy as my response hung in the room. His eyes lit up with a mix of surprise. In that charged moment, He leaned in slightly, his gaze holding mine. The soft glow of the desk lamps cast a warm halo around us as the city outside continued its bustling rhythm, unaware of the clandestine chapter unfolding within the office.

A daring spark ignited, and with a gentle brush of his fingers against mine, he closed the distance. Our lips met in a stolen kiss, a convergence of curiosity and desire. The office, once a canvas of routine, became a clandestine haven for shared secrets.

As the kiss lingered, the city lights outside blurred into a backdrop for this unexpected moment, a turning point in the story we were writing together.

Breaking the kiss, His eyes held a mixture of satisfaction and surprise. “I’ve wanted to do that for a long time,” he admitted his tone a whisper against the backdrop of the night.

A smile played on my lips as I replied, “Well, it seems desires were meant to be explored, especially when they’re as intriguing as yours.”

Eventually, we pulled away, our lips still tingling from the lingering kiss. The both of us smiled at each other, our eyes filled with warmth and love.

Blushing, I admitted, “Vedh, I didn’t expect that to happen, but I’m glad it did. I’m falling for you more and more every day.”

Grinning, He responded, “Aaditi, I feel the same way. Our love seems to grow stronger with each passing moment. You mean the world to me.”

Vedh dropped me home and planted a kiss on my forehead. As I entered her building, a sense of contentment lingered in my heart. The lingering taste of the kiss with Vedh still danced on my lips, filling me with joy.

The comforting thought of spending the day with Vedh, I trusted his confidant and the one who knew my soul deeply, brought a soft glow to my tired face. The memories of our hearty conversations, shared laughter, and the subtle gestures of understanding filled me with indescribable joy.

Leaning back against my seat, I closed my eyes for a moment, relishing the serenity that enveloped me. It was the contentment of being with someone who knew me intricately, the peace of being understood without words, that rejuvenated my spirit.

Though physically weary, my heart felt light, buoyed by the cherished memories of the day. The sheer bliss of spending time with Vedh, my cherished companion, had left an imprint of warmth and happiness that lingered, making the tiredness seem insignificant in comparison to the joy I felt.

Chapter 7
Pain and Tribulation

3 Weeks Later

The cafe buzzed with the low hum of conversations, but the atmosphere around my table felt like an impending storm. Vedh was running late, and I was lost in my thoughts, staring out the window, when the door opened with a jingle.

Aarav stood there, his presence alone sending a chill down my spine. The memories of a tumultuous past resurfaced, and I couldn't shake the feeling that trouble was imminent.

"Hello, Aaditi," Aarav said, a sinister smile playing on his lips. "Surprised to see me?"

I composed myself, squaring my shoulders. "What do you want, Aarav?"

He took a seat without waiting for an invitation, his eyes locked onto mine. "I've heard things, you know. About you and Vedh."

My jaw tightened. "What business is it of yours?"

He chuckled darkly. "Oh, babe, don't pretend you've forgotten everything. You and I... we had something special, didn't we?"

I took a deep breath, the scars of the past reopening. "We had something until you destroyed it."

His expression turned mocking. "I destroyed it? I seem to remember you pushing me away and now finding love in the arms of Vedh."

Anger flared within me. "You cheated on me, Aarav! You lied and betrayed my trust. You think that's not destructive?"

He leaned in, his voice a low hiss. "You were too naive to understand. I did what I had to do."

"I don't need your justifications," I shot back, my eyes blazing with intensity. "You ruined us, and I won't let you do it again."

His frustration poured out. "I thought we had something worth fighting for. I thought coming back would make you see that."

Sipping my coffee, I chose my words carefully. "Aarav, the past can't be erased. I've found a different path, a different kind of happiness. I can't go back."

His frustration manifested in restless gestures, the cafe's ambient noise providing a buffer for your intense conversation. "I won't let you forget what we had. You can't just erase me from your life."

"I'm not erasing you. But I can't let the past control my present. We both need to find our own paths."

His smile faded as he realized I wasn't the same person he could manipulate anymore. "I just wanted to see if you're genuinely happy with Vedh."

"I am," you said defiantly. "And unlike you, he values and respects me."

The tension in the air escalated, drawing the attention of nearby patrons. Aarav's face contorted with a mix of regret and frustration.

"You'll regret leaving me," he warned,

"I regret not leaving you sooner," I retorted, my voice unwavering.

"You remember our farewell day, don't you?" Aarav's tone carried a hint of nostalgia, but his eyes were searching for a reaction.

I met his gaze without flinching. "I remember it all too well."

"I was trapped," he began, his words dripping with an air of victimhood. "You never believed me. It was the day everything changed."

I scoffed, unable to contain my frustration. "Trapped? I saw what you did, Aarav. You made choices that ruined lives, including ours. Don't try to justify it now."

His face darkened with anger, and he leaned in closer. "You have no idea what I went through. You never gave me a chance to explain."

"What's there to explain?" I shot back, my patience wearing thin. "You made your choices, and now you have to live with the consequences."

Aarav's frustration boiled over. "You're so damn stubborn! I still love you, and you're not even willing to hear me out."

I shook my head, disbelief and disappointment mingling in my expression. "Love doesn't excuse what you did. And what you're doing now, trying to manipulate the past, is just as wrong. You had your chance, Aarav."

"Three years, Aaditi. I left everything, and you act like it meant nothing. Can't you see the chasing for love?"

"Aarav, love alone can't fix what happened. You left, and I had to find a way to heal. I can't go back to the way things were. We need to move on separately."

His eyes flashed with a mix of desperation and anger. "I'll prove you wrong. I'll make you see that there's more to the story than you know."

I stood my ground. "I've seen enough. Actions speak louder than words, Aarav, and yours spoke volumes. I won't let you disrupt my life again."

Him, realizing the futility of the argument, slammed his hand on the table in frustration. "You're making a mistake, Aaditi. But fine, if this is how you want it, be prepared to see the truth."

As Aarav walked away, the weight of the past seemed to lift. Vedh arrived just in time to see the tail end of the confrontation, and concern etched on his face.

"Everything okay?" Vedh asked, taking a seat beside me.

I took Vedh's hand, looking into his eyes with determination. "It is now."

Vedh's eyes searched mine, silently asking for an explanation. "Who was that?"

"Aarav," I said, a heavy sigh accompanying the name. "He came back, trying to reopen old wounds."

Vedh's expression hardened, a protective instinct surfacing. "What did he want?"

"He wanted to stir up the past, Vedh. But it's over now," I assured him, my gaze meeting him for his unwavering support.

As I recounted the encounter, Vedh's features shifted from concern to understanding and, finally, to determination. "You deserve peace, Aaditi. I won't let anyone disrupt that, and I'm here for you, no matter what. We'll face whatever comes our way together."

Just as Vedh spoke those reassuring words, his phone buzzed with an incoming call. He glanced at the screen, and a hint of concern crossed his face. "It's Mom," he said apologetically. "I should take this."

I nodded understandingly, and Vedh answered the call, his voice taking on a gentle tone as he engaged in a conversation with his mother. As he spoke, I observed the way his eyes softened, revealing a deep connection with his family.

As I waited for Vedh, my mind slipped into a cascade of thoughts. I found myself drawing comparisons between Vedh and Aarav, two individuals who couldn't have been more different in their approach toward life.

Vedh, with his gentle demeanor and understanding nature, had a way of calming turbulent waters. His politeness and empathy were constants, creating a space where conversations flowed easily, devoid of tension or discord. He listened, not just to reply but to truly understand, offering support without judgment. In his presence, I felt heard and cherished.

On the other hand, Aarav seemed unwavering and steadfast in his beliefs. His adamant nature often led to clashes, a rigidity that made compromise seem impossible. His assertiveness sometimes bordered on aggression, creating an atmosphere filled with tension and unease. Conversations with him were a battleground, each word carrying the weight of a potential conflict.

The contrast between their personalities was stark. Vedh's calmness was a soothing balm, a reassuring presence that made me feel safe and understood. His understanding of nature allowed for open discussions, fostering an environment where differences were embraced, not frowned upon.

Conversely, Aarav's aggressive stance seemed to fuel an atmosphere of contention. His insistence on his own beliefs overshadowed any possibility of finding common ground. The discomfort of being around such adamant energy lingered long after our interactions ended.

For me, the realization that Vedh was the one I wanted to share my life with came as a serene certainty, a truth that had settled deep within my heart. It was a clarity that needed no explanation or validation; it simply was.

In Vedh's presence, I found an undeniable comfort, a sense of completeness that extended beyond mere words. His understanding nature, his unwavering support, and the effortless way we connected on various levels resonated profoundly with me.

Every shared moment, every glance carried an unspoken depth—a silent language only we understood. I realized that it wasn't just about the calmness Vedh brought into my life but the way he effortlessly became an integral part of my happiness and aspirations.

On the other hand, there was Aarav. I found myself caught in a whirlwind of thoughts, each one circling around the incident involving Aarav. His actions on the farewell day lingered in my mind like an unresolved puzzle, each piece leaving an uncomfortable residue in my thoughts.

I replayed the scene in my mind, dissecting the details with a growing sense of discomfort. The more I reflected on it, the clearer it became that Aarav's behavior didn't align with my values or principles. It was a jarring realization, conflicting with the image I had of him and leaving me unsettled.

The discomfort persisted, creating a dissonance within me. I knew I needed to address my feelings and concerns, but I was unsure how to approach the subject. I found myself contemplating the implications of this incident on our relationship, torn between my feelings for Aarav and the undeniable discomfort caused by his actions.

After a while, Vedh concluded the call and returned his attention to me. "Sorry about that. Mom needed some advice about a family matter."

I smiled, understanding the importance of family and the commitments that came with it. "No need to apologize. Family comes first."

His gaze held a mixture of warmth and gratitude. "Thank you for understanding. Now, let's focus on us. Are you okay?"

His genuine concern melted away any lingering tension. "I am. Having you by my side makes everything better."

Vedh reached across the table, his hand finding mine. "We'll navigate through whatever comes our way together."

"Indeed, I was also thinking," I began with a smile, "how about we continue this evening at my place? I'd love to spend more time together before your family's trip to Pune."

Vedh's eyes lit up with enthusiasm. "That sounds perfect. I'd love to."

We paid the bill and made our way to my apartment. The city lights twinkled as we navigated the familiar streets, the anticipation of the evening ahead adding a touch of excitement to the air.

Once at my place, we decided to celebrate the upcoming milestones—my first day at the new office and Vedh's family trip—with a little impromptu gathering. We pulled out some snacks, uncorked a bottle of wine, and shared stories and dreams over the gentle clinking of glasses.

As the night progressed, we found ourselves immersed in the warmth of shared laughter, the glow of city lights outside casting a soft ambiance in the room. Vedh held my hand naturally, and we exchanged tender glances, letting the unspoken language of affection speak volumes.

In the quiet moments between conversations, we shared a sweet kiss. The room seemed to glow a little brighter, and the city outside faded into the background as we continued.

I also felt the need to be honest with Vedh about my past. Picture this: Aarav, the coldest dude in the emotional tundra, skating on the frozen surface of apathy while the rest of us were slipping and sliding in the slush of grief. His heart? Oh, it was locked up tighter than a safe filled with secrets.

He listened attentively, his eyes filled with understanding and concern. He reached out to hold my hand, offering comfort and support. "Aaditi," he said softly, "I'm here for you, and I appreciate your honesty. We'll face this together, and no matter what happens, our love will help us navigate any challenges."

As I spoke, the instances unfolded like chapters of a book, revealing the depth and nuances of our connection.

I remember one such instance:

Losing my mother was an indescribable pain, a void that seemed insurmountable. Amidst the anguish of her passing, there was an incident that lingered painfully in my memory - Aarav's obliviousness to my sorrow on that very day, his birthday.

My world was shattered, grief engulfing every moment, every breath. Yet, as the weight of my loss pressed upon me, Aarav's focus remained solely on his birthday celebration. His excitement and enthusiasm for his special day felt deafening against the backdrop of my silent agony.

His lack of acknowledgment and the absence of empathy during my darkest days left an indelible mark. In the midst of my mourning, I grappled with conflicting emotions. While part of me wished for his comfort, his presence, his obliviousness to my grief was a stark reminder of our emotional disconnect. It was a poignant moment that highlighted the stark contrast between our priorities, a moment when I realized that perhaps our emotional wavelengths did not sync as seamlessly as I had hoped.

The farewell day lingered as a haunting memory, its impact etched deep within me. I couldn't shake off the discomfort, the disheartening feeling of being misunderstood and unvalued, casting a shadow over my shared history with Aarav.

It wasn't just about that one moment; it was a culmination of unsettling incidents, each a fracture in the fabric of trust and camaraderie I had once cherished. I questioned the authenticity of our bond and the significance of our connection.

I longed for understanding, for someone to comprehend the turmoil within me. But in this moment of introspection, I realized that sometimes the greatest battles were fought silently, within the confines of one's own heart.

In the quiet depths of self-discovery, I found a version of myself I hadn't known before. The journey toward strength and confidence wasn't swift or effortless; it was a collection of moments, lessons learned, and choices made.

I vividly recall the shifts within me, moments where I stood firm against the tides of uncertainty and where I chose to confront challenges head-on. It was a conscious decision, a promise to myself—a commitment to prioritize my well-being, my dreams, and my happiness.

Vedh (concerned): I'm sorry you had to go through that. But please remember, his presence doesn't change anything between us. We are stronger together, and I'm here to support you no matter what. He wrapped his arms around me for a while.

I'm grateful, and I know I'm so lucky to have you by my side. Your love and understanding mean the world to me. Let's not let Aarav's actions affect us or our relationship.

In the comfort of my bedroom, Vedh and I find a moment to share an intimate connection. With a subtle glance and unspoken understanding, he takes my hand, leading me to the soft embrace of the bed. The atmosphere is charged with anticipation.

Without a word, Vedh pulls me close, his hands exploring the contours of my body. The chemistry between us intensifies as we share lingering glances and gentle caresses. There's an unspoken agreement that ignites a fire between us.

"We're supposed to take it slow," I whisper, although my voice carries a tone of desire rather than protest.

Vedh stills, gazing deeply into my eyes. "Who said we can't enjoy the journey, one intimate moment at a time?"

Vedh smirks, his eyes reflecting a mix of passion and playfulness. He leans in, capturing my lips in a hungry kiss. The world outside the bedroom fades away as we give in to the magnetic pull of each other running his nose down the length of mine, and placing soft kisses at the corners of my mouth. We exchange a wordless agreement, and he releases one of my hands, clasping my chin to hold me still while his tongue explores my mouth. I surrender to the passionate exchange.

"You know," he begins, his voice a gentle caress, "there's something about being here with you that feels like love is in the air."

A soft smile plays on my lips as I respond, "It does, doesn't it? Like our own little sanctuary away from the world."

Without uttering a word, Vedh leans in, his lips meeting mine in a hungry kiss. The room seems to disappear, leaving only the echo of our shared breaths

Breaking the kiss, he murmurs against my lips, "I've dreamt of this moment."

I chuckle softly, "Me too, Vedh. Me too."

Shifting positions, he moves between my legs, his hand sliding beneath my skirt. No need for words; our desires are communicated through touch. Vedh's fingers create an electrifying sensation, weaving a sensual spell that leaves me yearning for more.

A seductive twinkle in his eye. "Do you want me, Aaditi?"

His question hangs in the air, charged with desire. I meet his intense gaze, feeling the anticipation build. With a mischievous smile, I respond, "What do you think, Vedh?" My voice carries a playful tone, teasing him as I revel in the moment. as his lips curve into a wicked smile. He withdraws his hand briefly, tracing my lips with his index finger before pushing it into my mouth, mimicking our earlier exchange. Vedh shifts between my legs again, his hips moving rhythmically, the fabric of my skirt rubbing provocatively.

"Is this what you want?" he murmurs, his voice low and husky.

"Yes," I moan, abandoning any pretense of resistance.

His hand returns beneath my skirt, teeth scraping along my jaw. "Do you realize how irresistible you are, Aaditi?" His voice is hoarse as he rocks against me. I try to respond but end up groaning loudly. Vedh captures my mouth again, tugging at my bottom lip before plunging his tongue into my mouth.

"Do you enjoy my touch?" I whisper.

His brow furrows briefly, and he stops grinding. "Of course, Aaditi. Your touch is my sanctuary, a moment of respite from the chaos of the world." His voice hums with passionate sincerity.

Kneeling between my legs, Vedh swiftly removes my blouse, leaving me in my casual clothes. He follows jeans, discarding his shirt. Pulling me onto his lap, he clasps his arms just above my waist.

"Touch me," he breathes, and I comply without hesitation.

My fingers tentatively brush through his hair and over his strong shoulders. He inhales sharply, pupils dilating with a sensual response to my touch. As my fingers explore, he watches intently. Leaning forward, I plant soft kisses on his chest, feeling the hard, sculpted lines of sinew and muscle.

"I want you," he murmurs, giving the green light to our desires. My fingers tangle in his hair, pulling his head back to claim his mouth. Fire ignites in my belly. He groans, pushing me back onto the bed. Ripping off my skirt, undoing his fly simultaneously.

"Bedroom rendezvous," he whispers, swiftly sealing the deal. I groan, and he stills, grabbing my face between his hands.

"I love you, Aaditi," he murmurs, and we surrender to the magnetic pull of desire, the bedroom becoming an intimate haven amidst the chaos of the world.

The evening concluded with a promise to stay connected despite the physical distance we would be facing for few weeks. As Vedh bid farewell, the anticipation of my first day at the office mixed with the warmth of the evening spent together, creating a tapestry of emotions that would linger in the air, marking the beginning of a new chapter in both our lives.

The early light of my first day as an intern peeked through the curtains, casting a hopeful glow at the beginning of a new chapter. Brimming in excitement, I decided to share the morning with my dad, choosing to savor a simple breakfast before setting out for the office. We sat at the table, and my dad looked at me with a fatherly curiosity.

My dad's curiosity broke the silence, "What's the special occasion for this early start?"

With a smile, I shared, "First day at the office, Dad. I thought we could have breakfast together before I head out."

Nodding in approval, Dad remarked, "Oh yes! A good way to start the day, and all the best for your first day. It's been a while since we had a quiet morning like this."

As we prepared to leave, the car became the vessel for both conversation and contemplation.

Curious, Dad said, "I noticed someone was here last night. Who was it?"

Grinning, I thought, "Shit, I hope he was not here when we were busy with our thing!" I lied and confessed.

I fidgeted nervously, my cheeks turning a shade of pink. "Uh, yeah, Dad. A friend stopped by. We were just catching up."

Dad's gaze lingered for a moment, then he chuckled. "Friend, huh? I saw someone in the lift leaving our house late night. Seemed like more than just catching up."

My heart skipped a beat as I tried to maintain composure. "Oh, that? Yeah, that was Vedh. We were... hanging out. You know, nothing serious." "Raising an eyebrow, Dad inquired, "Vedh, huh? Nice guy?"

With a nod, I affirmed, "Yeah, he's a really nice guy. In fact, I kind of like him."

The mention of Vedh prompted a shift in my dad's expression from curiosity to concern - a protective instinct surfacing.

Concerned, he said, "Aaditi, I just want you to be careful. I don't want you to go through any heartbreak or troubles."

Assuring him, I responded, "Don't worry, Dad. Vedh is a good friend, and we're taking things slow. I appreciate your concern, though."

He nodded and then offered a parting wish as we neared the office.

Smiling, he said, "Aaditi, I know you'll do great on your first day. Just remember to take things one step at a time. Wishing you all the best, my dear."

His words carried a blend of pride and warmth, a father's blessing encapsulated in a simple yet profound wish. With gratitude in my heart, I stepped out of the car, ready to embrace the new challenges that awaited me, fueled by the encouragement and support of those who cared.

The office buzzed with a symphony of ringing phones and the rhythmic hum of workstations. I stepped into the world of marketing, my new domain, as a marketing intern. The walls adorned with charts and graphs painted a vibrant picture of strategic campaigns, and the air was charged with the energy of creativity and innovation.

Assigned to a desk amidst the hustle, I marveled at the organized chaos that defined the marketing department. Colleagues exchanged ideas and collaborated on projects, and the atmosphere resonated with the dynamic rhythm of the corporate world.

However, there was a unique twist to my journey. My dad and I had made a conscious decision not to disclose our familial connection within the office. In this professional arena, I was to be treated as just another employee. This decision added an element of mystery to my interactions, allowing me to navigate the challenges of the workplace independently.

During my lunch break, a call from the reception piqued my curiosity. As I made my way to pick up the unexpected delivery, there it was—a delicious-looking lunch sent over by Vedh, accompanied by a note that held a touch of sweetness.

In elegant, the note read: ***Hoping your first day is as amazing as you! I love you, and I'm rooting for your success. May each moment bring you joy, and may the challenges only make you stronger. Looking forward to hearing all about your day. Yours always, Vedh.***

Life found its rhythm in the following months. Vedh became a constant, whether it was just the two of us or with friends like Sarah. Aarav, since our confrontation, faded away from my life.

A secret joy was sharing moments with my dad at the office, blending work and bonding in a unique way. These relationships brought stability and joy, creating a mosaic of simple, shared moments that defined this chapter of my life.

7 Months later

I opened my eyes, yawning and stretching, and then made my way to the bathroom to kick start my day. I saw Vedh's messages that he had already headed off to work; since I had the day off, a leisurely shower was first on my list. After the shower, I went to my closet, and just as I was reaching for my favorite pair of worn jeans, I had an idea. "Brilliant!" I smiled to myself as I reached for a crisp, semi-sheer white blouse, a black pencil skirt, and black heels. I walked to the dresser and pulled out a sexy black lacy bra, matching thong, a garter belt, and a black seamed hose. "There! This should do it!" I mused to myself.

I took one last long look in the mirror.... The top three buttons were undone... check. Cleavage showing... check. Looking damn hot... oh yeah, check. I was ready. All the way to Vedh's office, I thought about what I planned to do. I had been teasing him for months, threatening to walk into the office and seduce him in front of everyone. I fantasized about it a lot. "Well, here I am, baby," I said out loud as I pulled into his office parking lot.

Exiting the elevator, I opened the door. When I saw all the cubicles where his team sat, I had a moment of fear. "Aaditi can pull this off," I whispered to myself nervously. Vedh's glass-enclosed office was across the room. I saw him sitting at his desk, on the phone. "Yes, go review the files..."

I slowly started walking down the aisle that led to his office. Maybe it was our connection, maybe it was a coincidence, but at that exact moment, Vedh looked up and saw me slowly striding his way. He disconnected the phone, stood up, and walked to his side wall, leaning against it. He crossed his arms and smiled. Then his jaw dropped.

Without stopping, I closed the door behind me and started unbuttoning the rest of her blouse until it was fully open. I let it drop to the floor. My barely lacy bra jutting my tits out. His assistant on the phone next to her coughed and then forgot about his client as she stared as she could view his office door. Next, I reached behind my back and unzipped skirt. It slid down, and I stepped out of it, tossing it on the floor. By now, it was the shock and admiration on Vedh's face that put all my fears to rest. I was just getting started when he drew the curtain of his glass office.

As I moved closer, he looked at me up and down… bra, panties, garter, heels. I knew his cock was swelling even before I saw the growing bulge in his pants. I giggled as I reached Vedh. I picked up his landline and called his assistant, who sat at her desk with her mouth agape. "Hold his calls, please," I told her sweetly and disconnected immediately.

Because it was a glass office, it offered little privacy, but it was quiet except for the music being piped in. I could, however, still hear the buzz from the employees outside his office, craning to get a glimpse. I stood before Vedh and put my arms around his neck, leaned forward and nuzzled his ear. "Did you like my surprise?" He kissed me passionately and said, "I loved it. You are looking so hot right now!"

Vedh and I used to engage in a lot of sexting, especially on the days when he was away for business trips. Our messages became a playful and intimate way to connect, bridging the physical distance between us with shared desires and fantasies. It added a layer of excitement and anticipation to our communication, creating a special connection even when we couldn't be together in person. And finally, I decided to give in to this fantasy that once he had shared with me.

I used one leg to push him apart and then pressed my body against him. He groaned as his hands found mine and moved seductively over my body. He unbuttoned my bra, and it fell to the floor. My hard nipples screamed for his attention, which he willingly gave. Vedh bent down and sucked them one at a time, causing me to throw back my head and squeal in delight. I reached down and undid his belt buckle, thrusting my hand down his trousers and grabbing his hard swollen cock.

While I stroked him, He undid his trousers and let them fall to the floor next to my bra. I slid down on my knees and took his cock in my mouth. Vedh was vaguely aware of the curious eyes staring into the office. But, His focus was on this sexual tigress in front of him... Awestruck, she could give head, he thought to himself with bliss. As I touched him, licked him, and sucked him, he ran his fingers through my long hair and used every ounce of willpower he had not to cum… right then, right there. I was driving him wild. The way I flick my tongue, teasing his cock, my lips closing around him, pulling him deeper and deeper down my throat.

Because I knew he was about to cum, I stopped, laid back on the floor, and stared up at him. I raised my hand and, with one finger, motioned for him to "come here.' Damn, I was sexy. Vedh mounted me and pushed his throbbing cock inside me. He wasn't gentle, he was fucking horny. I moaned his name. That turned him on. He thrust his cock deeply inside my pussy. I curved my back and met him thrust to thrust. "Fuck! Aaditi," Vedh cried out. "Fuck me, baby," I replied hoarsely.

"Oh, baby! Aaditi! Aaditi!" We revealed pleasure as a sensation that spread. It was breathtaking. "Vedh, you were amazing!" I exclaimed, trying to calm myself. "No, baby, you were the pure bliss of my day! I love you so much. I'm incredibly fortunate to have a girlfriend who can fulfill my fantasies." He sealed his words with a kiss.

Exiting Vedh's office hand in hand, the remnants of our intimate encounter clung to the night air. As we neared the parking lot, a seemingly trivial parking dispute erupted into an ominous confrontation with a mysterious figure.

"Who is this guy, Vedh? What's happening?" I asked, eyeing the stranger with unease.

Vedh, attempting to defuse the situation, remained unaware of the figure's unsettling fixation. "I've seen him before, Vedh—near the college and outside the gym. It's not just about parking. Something's off about him," I whispered urgently.

Realization flashed in Vedh's eyes as the pieces connected. The stranger's presence had woven itself into the fabric of our recent experiences.

As we retreated, Vedh, now more alert, offered, "I'll drop you home." His reassuring squeeze spoke volumes as we navigated the night, the shadows of uncertainty looming over our shared intimacy.

Chapter 8
Caught Red Handed

(Flashback)

I couldn't believe it was finally our farewell day. It was a day filled with excitement, nostalgia, and the bittersweet feeling of parting ways with my high school friends. But there was one person I wanted to see before the celebrations began - Aarav.

We had made plans to meet in the college's cafeteria that morning. We had even chatted about it the night before, both looking forward to spending a few moments together before the official holiday started. I had been eagerly waiting for this day, and seeing Aarav was an essential part of it.

As the clock ticked closer to our agreed meeting time, I couldn't contain my excitement. I sent Aarav a text message, "Hey, Aarav, are you on your way to college? Can't wait to see you!" I waited anxiously for his reply, but there was nothing. No text, no notification. It was strange; Aarav was usually prompt in responding to my messages.

I decided to give it a few more minutes, thinking he might be running late. But as time passed and there was still no response, worry began to creep in. What could be keeping him? Did he forget our plans? I couldn't shake the feeling that something was off.

With each passing minute, my anxiety grew. I messaged him again, "Aarav, where are you? We were supposed to meet at the cafeteria." Still, no response. It was as if he had vanished into thin air.

The farewell event was a whirlwind of emotions. There were smiles, tears, and laughter as we celebrated the end of our high school journey and prepared to step into a new chapter of our lives. Colorful decorations adorned the venue, and the air was filled with excitement and nostalgia. It was a day that we had all been eagerly anticipating, but for me, there was a cloud of worry hanging over it.

As I moved through the crowd of my friends and classmates, my eyes scanned the faces, hoping to catch a glimpse of Aarav. He was supposed to be here, by my side, sharing this important day with me. But he was nowhere to be seen, and my concern grew with each passing minute.

Finally, I spotted Sarah and hurried over to her. My footsteps quickened, my heart racing with worry. When I reached her, I couldn't hide the anxiety that was etched across my face. I took a deep breath and said, "Sarah," my voice trembling with concern, "I can't find Aarav anywhere. He was supposed to be here, and he's not answering my calls or messages. I'm really worried about him."

Her eyes mirrored my concern as she listened to my words. The noise of the celebration faded into the background as we stood there, contemplating what to do next. It was supposed to be a joyous occasion, but Aarav's absence cast a shadow over the day, and I knew that finding him had become our top priority.

As Sarah and I stood there, with no response from Aarav's phone, we exchanged a determined look. It was clear that something unusual was happening, and we couldn't afford to wait any longer. We needed to find Aarav and make sure he was okay.

"Sarah, we can't just stand here waiting. Let's go to Aarav's house and check if he's there. Maybe something urgent came up, and he couldn't make it to the farewell."

She replied worryingly, "You're right, Aaditi. Let's go see if he's at home. If he's not, maybe someone there can give us some information about where he might be."

With a sense of purpose, we quickly made our way to the parking lot, located my car, and hopped in. The drive to Aarav's house was filled with a tense silence as we both contemplated what could be going on. Our worry for our friend hung heavy in the air, and we hoped that we would find answers once we reached his home.

As Sarah and I made our way toward Aarav's house, the urgency of the situation weighed on us. We knew we needed the help of our friends to find Aarav and unravel the mystery of his sudden disappearance on our farewell day. I reached for my phone and dialed the numbers of our friends, Hemakshi, Monish, and Rudhay.

I could feel my fingers dancing nervously on the phone's screen as I dialed each number, the air inside the car thick with tension. Sarah's eyes mirrored the unease that gnawed at me.

I spoke, my voice shaky with worry. "Sarah, let's call Hemakshi, Monish, and Rudhay. We need to assemble the gang to help us find Aarav."

Sarah nodded, understanding the gravity of the situation. "Absolutely. The more eyes we have searching for him, the better our chances of finding him."

Each ring felt like an eternity, and when Hemakshi finally picked up, relief washed over me, only to be replaced by urgency.

Hemakshi's voice crackled through the phone speaker. "Hey, what's up?"

I conveyed my concern. "Hemakshi, it's Aarav. He's missing from the farewell, and he's not responding to calls or messages. We need your help to find him. Can you come to Aarav's house?"

Hemakshi's response was immediate and alarmed. "Oh my god! I'll be there right away!"

As Hemakshi pledged her support, the next call to Monish echoed with heightened anxiety.

Monish's voice came through, tinged with concern. "Hey, what's going on?"

I shared my anxiety. "Monish, it's Aarav. He's not here, and we're really worried. Can you come to Aarav's house to help us search for him?"

Monish assured me, "Of course. I'm on my way."

But the absence of Rudhay's response added a layer of uncertainty.

Sarah voiced the concern that hung in the air. "Aaditi, Rudhay isn't picking up. Should we wait for him, or should we go ahead and assemble the others?"

I was visibly worried, so I made a decisive call. "We can't afford to wait, Sarah. Let's go to Aarav's house, and if Rudhay can catch up with us, that would be great. But we can't delay this any longer."

The tires hummed on the asphalt as the car cut through the night, the ominous nature of our mission hanging thick in the air. With the support of Hemakshi and Monish and the lingering hope for Rudhay's arrival, I sped toward Aarav's house, determined to unravel the unsettling mystery that surrounded our missing friend.

Sarah and I exchanged concerned glances as we stood in front of Aarav's house. There was an eerie stillness about the place, and it sent shivers down my spine. We had come here hoping to find Aarav and get an explanation for his sudden disappearance on our farewell day, but there was no sign of him anywhere.

Sarah nodded in agreement, and together, we approached Aarav's house for help. My heart was pounding, and I was desperate for any information about Aarav's whereabouts. I asked, "Excuse me, do you know where Aarav is? We were supposed to meet him, but he's not responding to our calls or messages."

The house help, a middle-aged woman with a worried expression, looked at us with sympathy. She said, "I'm sorry, but Aarav received an anonymous call early this morning, and he left in a hurry. He seemed very tense and didn't say where he was going, but I overheard him mention something about Sector 29 in Gurgaon."

My heart sank at the news. Gurgaon was quite a distance from here, and for Aarav to leave without telling anyone was deeply concerning. Why would he receive an anonymous call on our farewell day? What could have happened to make him leave like that? I knew we had to find him and make sure he was okay.

Sarah and I, accompanied by Hemakshi and Monish, decided to travel to Gurgaon in order to find Aarav. Our concern deepened when there was still no sign of Aarav. We searched the immediate vicinity and even asked Aarav's neighbors, but no one had seen him. It was as if he had vanished without a trace.

Just when our anxiety was reaching its peak, my phone buzzed, and I saw Rudhay's name on the screen. With trembling hands, I answered the call.

Rudhay's voice, slightly out of breath, echoed through the phone. "Hey, Aaditi. I'm in Gurgaon."

I was bewildered. "Gurgaon? Rudhay, what are you doing in Gurgaon on our farewell day?"

Rudhay hesitated. "I... I had some personal stuff to take care of. Look, it's not important right now. Have you found Aarav?"

Puzzled, I responded, "No, Rudhay, we haven't. He's missing, and we're really worried. We were at his house trying to figure out where he could be. Can't explain everything to you on call. We're all traveling to Gurgaon. We got a lead from Aarav's house help."

Concerned, Rudhay offered, "I'll meet you at MG Road. Just keep looking for Aarav, and I'll explain everything when I get there."

After hanging up, I was still perplexed by Rudhay's sudden trip to Gurgaon on a day like this. But I couldn't dwell on it for long. Finding Aarav was our top priority, and his well-being had to come first.

Addressing the group, I said, "Rudhay is in Gurgaon for some reason, but he's returning. Right now, let's focus on finding Aarav. We can sort out everything else later."

The group nodded in agreement, and we continued our search for Aarav, our worries deepening with each passing moment.

As we anxiously waited for Rudhay at the MG Road station, the tension in the group was palpable. We kept dialing Aarav's number repeatedly, desperately hoping for a response, but there was still no answer. The worry and uncertainty were overwhelming, and I couldn't hold back my tears any longer.

Emotions took over as tears streamed down my face, a wave of sadness and fear washing over me. It was difficult to comprehend how Aarav, our close friend, could be missing on a day as significant as our farewell.

Sarah, always the pillar of support, put her arm around me, offering comfort as the others in the group tried to console me.

"Gentle and reassuring," Sarah said, "Aaditi, we're all here for you. We'll find Aarav, I promise. He'll be okay."

Hemakshi, Monish, and Rudhay joined in, offering words of encouragement and support, reassuring me that we would do everything in our power to locate Aarav.

Rudhay, speaking firmly, said, "Aaditi, we're not giving up. Let's go to the authorities and file a missing person report. We'll leave no stone unturned until we find Aarav."

Their comforting words and determination helped me regain my composure, and I wiped away my tears. We knew we had a challenging task ahead, but with our close-knit group working together, we were determined to find Aarav.

Out of nowhere, we received a call from Aarav's number. My eyes lit up as I saw Aarav's name flashing on my phone screen. However, it wasn't Aarav on the phone, and what happened next left me in shock and utter disbelief.

A deep voice, unfamiliar and stern, spoke on the other end of the line. It was Inspector Hamid Khan of the Gurgaon Police, and his words sent a chill down my spine.

Inspector Khan's voice on the other end of the line pierced through the air, "Is this Aaditi?"

My heart skipped a beat as I replied, "Yes, this is Aaditi. Is Aarav okay? Where is he?"

"I'm calling from Aarav's phone. I'm afraid Aarav is in a very serious situation right now. We found him at The Umrao Hotel in Gurgaon. He's here, but he's in custody," Inspector Khan revealed.

My heart sank, and my mind raced with a million questions. What could have possibly happened to Aarav?

Desperation seeped into my voice as I asked, "What happened? Is he hurt? Why is he in custody?"

Inspector Khan hesitated before delivering the unsettling news, "Aarav was found in a compromising situation with a woman at the hotel. She is unconscious, and both of them are naked. Furthermore, a video of Aarav in this compromising position has been uploaded online."

The shock and disbelief were overwhelming. I couldn't process the information. Aarav, my friend, was in a dire situation, and the gravity of the allegations against him was staggering. I felt a mix of emotions—confusion, anger, and deep concern for Aarav.

"I... I don't understand. This can't be true. We need to come to Gurgaon immediately. Please, tell us where he is," I pleaded, desperately wanting to unravel the truth behind the bewildering turn of events.

At that moment, my friends gathered around, their faces mirroring the shock and concern etched across mine. Hemakshi and Monish exchanged worried glances, their silence amplifying the gravity of the news. Sarah, always the pillar of strength, stood by me with a reassuring hand on my shoulder.

Hemakshi's voice, filled with concern and support, reached my ears, "Aaditi, we're here for you. We need to head to Gurgaon and get to the bottom of this."

Monish, ever steadfast, chimed in, "Absolutely. Let's not waste any time. We'll face whatever it is together."

Sarah, with unwavering loyalty, declared, "Aarav is our friend, and we'll support him. No matter what, we're in this together."

As our group hastily made our way to the Gurgaon Police Station, the atmosphere was thick with tension and uncertainty. The journey felt like an eternity, each passing moment overshadowed by the gravity of the situation involving our friend Aarav.

Upon arriving at the police station, the imposing structure loomed before us, its cold, gray exterior a stark contrast to the warmth we sought within. With every step, my heart pounded, the echoes of Inspector Khan's revelations still resonating in my mind.

Entering the station, the sterile scent of disinfectant clung to the air. A sense of foreboding enveloped us as we approached the front desk. An officer behind the counter, engrossed in paperwork, looked up as we approached.

The officer behind the desk looked up, inquiring, “Can I help you?”

With a sense of urgency, I replied, “Yes, we’re here about our friend, Aarav. Inspector Hamid Khan contacted us and informed us about his situation.”

The officer’s gaze shifted from curiosity to a more measured understanding as he directed us to a waiting area. The cold metal chairs offered little comfort as we settled in, exchanging anxious glances while the clock on the wall ticked away the seconds.

After what felt like an eternity, Inspector Khan emerged from a corridor, his expression grave. We rose from our seats, anticipation, and anxiety etched on our faces.

Inspector Khan: “I appreciate your prompt arrival. Follow me.”

Our group followed him down a series of hallways, the clatter of our footsteps echoing through the sterile corridors. As we entered a room marked “Interrogation Room,” my apprehension intensified. Aarav sat inside, his face a canvas of conflicting emotions—shock, confusion, and a hint of relief at the sight of familiar faces.

Inspector Khan, sitting across from us, maintained a stoic expression as he delved into the disturbing narrative.

His voice, solemn and laden with troubling information, filled the room, “The video was uploaded to a popular social media platform, and it quickly gained traction. In it, Aarav and the woman were found in a compromising situation at The Umrao Hotel. The woman alleges misconduct, and the video has sparked a public outcry."

A heavy silence settled over the room, each word sinking in with the weight of an anvil. Aarav's face mirrored the disbelief and shock etched on ours.

"I swear, I have no idea how this happened. I don't even remember being in such a situation with anyone," Aarav exclaimed, his words reflecting the genuine confusion that painted his expression.

Inspector Khan continued, "We understand this is a lot to process. Our initial investigation suggests that the woman involved has filed a formal complaint, and we are duty-bound to conduct a thorough inquiry."

The implications of the situation began to unfold like a twisted puzzle, with each piece revealing more complexity. I couldn't fathom how Aarav, someone I knew so well, could be entangled in such a bewildering web.

"Inspector, there has to be some mistake. Aarav wouldn't willingly get involved in something like this. Is there any way we can prove his innocence?" I questioned, desperation lacing my words.

Inspector Khan nodded, acknowledging the gravity of the situation, "We are gathering evidence, including statements from witnesses and hotel staff. A forensic team is also examining the video to establish its authenticity. But be aware, social media has a way of amplifying things, and public opinion can be unforgiving."

As we absorbed the information, a surge of determination replaced the initial shock. A shared understanding formed among us — we needed to uncover the truth, not just for Aarav's sake but to restore justice and salvage his reputation.

The startling discovery of scratch marks on Aarav's body and the unexpected identity of the girl, our classmate Naina, left us all bewildered. It was an alarming twist that we struggled to comprehend, and it was imperative to delve deeper into the circumstances.

As we gathered at the police station, a cloud of uncertainty hung over us. Aarav, a friend we thought we knew well, and Naina, a familiar face from our class, found themselves entangled in a deeply troubling situation. The allegations cast a shadow on our understanding of the people involved.

The police began their inquiries, and both Aarav and Naina recounted their versions of the events. The atmosphere was charged with tension as we listened attentively.

Aarav vigorously denied the accusations, explaining that the fog of intoxication had erased his memory of the incident. He was perplexed and shocked to find himself in a compromising situation alongside Naina.

On the other hand, Naina appeared distressed as she recounted the sequence of events leading up to the incident. She described how Aarav had offered her a drink, leading to her state of intoxication, and claimed that she had experienced an uncomfortable encounter with him. In her distress, she mentioned the scratches on Aarav's body, which had resulted from her attempts to protect herself.

The gravity of the situation weighed heavily on us. We were caught between our loyalty to Aarav and our concern for Naina, who had leveled a serious accusation. It was a deeply disconcerting and complex moment, and we understood that the authorities would need to conduct a thorough investigation to unveil the truth. Aarav claimed that he had woken up alongside Naina in bewilderment, not comprehending how they had ended up in such an uncomfortable situation.

The incident's aftermath sent shockwaves through our school, as it had become a media sensation. The school authorities were understandably concerned and demanded an explanation for what had transpired. They wanted to ensure the safety and well-being of all students.

However, a surprising turn of events unfolded when Aarav's father intervened. He chose to settle the matter with the school authorities and the police, using financial means to do so. It appeared that he wished to protect his son from further scrutiny and the potential consequences of the case.

As a result of this settlement, Aarav's name was removed from the case, and the police were asked to close the matter. This decision left many of us bewildered and disheartened, as it prioritized financial settlements over a thorough investigation and justice for all parties involved.

The incident remained clouded in mystery, and the truth of what had actually happened that night continued to elude us. It was a stark reminder of how power and influence could influence the course of justice, leaving many unanswered questions and a lingering sense of injustice among those directly or indirectly affected by the incident.

The incident left me in a state of profound confusion and emotional turmoil. The settlement and Aarav's removal from the case had raised many questions in my mind. I couldn't help but feel betrayed, as it seemed that Aarav had managed to evade the consequences of the allegations against him.

As a result, I made the painful decision not to talk to Aarav. I simply couldn't bring myself to trust him or believe his side of the story. The events of that night and the subsequent actions of Aarav's father had cast a dark shadow over our friendship, leaving me feeling hurt and uncertain.

The sense of betrayal and confusion weighed heavily on my heart. It would take time for me to come to terms with what had happened and to decide how to move forward in my relationship with Aarav, if at all. The trust that had once been the foundation of our friendship had been deeply shaken, and I needed time and clarity to navigate these complex emotions.

The emotional turmoil I experienced after the incident continued to haunt me. My feelings for Aarav were undeniable, and I desperately wanted to believe that he was innocent, that the person I knew could never have been involved in such a situation. However, doubts and suspicions persisted in my mind, making it difficult to reconcile the Aarav I knew with the allegations that had been made against him.

Naina's decision to drop all charges and leave the city only added to the confusion. It was a puzzling turn of events, leaving us all with more questions than answers. Her sudden departure created an air of mystery around the entire situation, making it even harder to discern the truth.

A few days later, news came that Naina had committed suicide. She could not bear the shame of being raped and assaulted by one of her classmates.

The news that Naina had allegedly committed suicide following the alleged assault by Aarav was a devastating revelation. It added an unbearable weight of tragedy to the already complex and troubling situation.

The word "assault" cast a dark shadow over the circumstances surrounding Naina's death, making it an even more distressing and somber event. The news left us all in a state of profound sadness and disbelief as we tried to come to terms with the shocking turn of events.

The school community's reaction was harsh and swift. Aarav was demonized, and his reputation was tarnished beyond repair. It was as if he had already been judged and sentenced by our peers, and I couldn't help but feel a deep sense of sadness for him, even as I grappled with my own conflicted feelings.

The incident had left a profound impact on all of us, and it was a stark reminder of how complex and delicate matters of justice and truth could be. As time passed, I found myself unable to fully move on from the turmoil, trapped between my love for Aarav and the doubts that continued to linger in my mind.

The prayer meeting for Naina following her tragic suicide was a somber and emotional gathering that brought together all of us friends who had known her. It was a moment of collective mourning and reflection on the loss of someone who had been a part of our lives.

Yet, despite the shared grief, there was a palpable uneasiness in the air, a cloud of unresolved questions and simmering tensions. The shadow of what had happened on that fateful day hung heavy over the gathering.

Many of us couldn't help but harbor suspicions about Aarav's involvement, given the allegations made against him. The whispers and hushed conversations among us hinted at the belief that he bore some responsibility for Naina's tragic end. However, there was a pervasive sense of resignation, an acknowledgment that Aarav's influential father would likely shield him from any significant consequences.

The weight of this knowledge—the feeling that justice might never be served—added to the complex emotions of the prayer meeting. It was a moment of collective grief and a painful reminder of how the events of that day had forever altered our lives, leaving us with a sense of injustice that was difficult to reconcile.

As we paid our respects to Naina, the uneasiness in the air was a reflection of the unresolved questions and the deep sorrow that had come to define this chapter of our lives.

The profound grief and anger that consumed Naina's mother in the wake of her daughter's tragic suicide were all too understandable. The loss of a child is an unimaginable pain, and it was only natural for her to seek justice and retribution for what she believed had transpired.

Her fervent desire for Aarav to face the most severe punishment—hanging—was a reflection of the depth of her anguish and the conviction that she held regarding his alleged involvement in Naina's death.

However, the reality of the situation weighed heavily on all of us who had known Naina and had been connected to the events of that day. The knowledge that Aarav's father's influence and resources might protect him from facing the full consequences of the allegations created a sense of resignation among us.

It was a painful realization that the pursuit of justice could be compromised by power and privilege, leaving us with a lingering sense of injustice that was difficult to reconcile. Despite the intensity of emotions and the fervent desire for accountability, many of us knew that the road to justice in this case would be fraught with challenges and uncertainty.

The weeks following the incident were fraught with tension, and my heartbreak was a palpable presence. As I distanced myself from Aarav, the silence between us grew heavy with the weight of unspoken words and shattered trust.

One evening, as the sun dipped below the horizon, casting long shadows across the deserted school courtyard, I found myself sitting alone on a bench, wrestling with conflicting emotions. Aarav approached hesitantly, his eyes reflecting the turmoil within.

"Aarav, I can't do this. I can't just act like everything's okay," I said, my voice barely above a whisper.

He took a deep breath, his gaze fixed on the ground. "I know I messed up, and I'm not expecting you to just forgive me. I just need you to hear me out."

I nodded, signaling for him to continue.

He began recounting the events of that ill-fated night, the fog of intoxication clouding his memory. He spoke of bewilderment and shock at finding himself entangled in a compromising situation with Naina. As he spoke, remorse etched across his face, I couldn't help but sense the sincerity in his words.

"I messed up, and I can't change that. But I never wanted to hurt you, and I certainly didn't want any harm to come to Naina," He confessed, his eyes pleading for understanding.

I sighed. My emotions were still a tumultuous sea. "Aarav, how do I know you're not just saying this to ease your guilt? Naina's gone, and there are so many unanswered questions."

Aarav looked directly into my eyes, the weight of the situation etched on his face. "I wish I had all the answers, but I don't. What I do know is that I need to make things right. I need to change, learn from this, and be a better person. And I want you to be a part of that journey."

I remained silent for a moment, the gravity of his words sinking in. The pain in Aarav's eyes mirrored my own, and for the first time, I saw vulnerability in him.

"I don't know if I can trust you again, Aarav," I admitted, my voice breaking.

He nodded, acknowledging the difficulty of the situation. "I understand. I just want you to know that I'm not giving up on us. I'll do whatever it takes to earn back your trust."

Aarav sighed, his shoulders slumping slightly. "I get it. I messed up, and I understand why it's hard for you to believe me. But I swear, I never meant for any of this to happen. I want to make things right, not just for us but for everyone involved."

His words sounded sincere, yet a lingering doubt persisted. The events leading up to this moment had been marked by confusion, betrayal, and an unsettling sense of injustice. Aarav's attempts to mend our relationship clashed with the unresolved mystery surrounding Naina's departure and tragic end.

"I need time, Aarav," I said, the weight of my emotions evident in my voice. "I can't just pretend everything is okay, and I can't trust you right now. There's too much we don't know about that night, and I can't ignore the doubts in my mind."

Aarav nodded, understanding the gravity of the situation. "I don't expect you to forgive me right away. I just want a chance to prove that I'm serious about changing and making amends."

He walked away, and a sense of emptiness lingered in the courtyard. The rift between us seemed insurmountable, and my heart remained guarded against the possibility of further disappointment.

As time passed, Aarav's life took a different trajectory. He moved to Mumbai and sought opportunities that were far removed from the events that had transpired in our school days. His desire for a fresh start led him to request his father to send him abroad for further studies, putting distance between him and the past.

Despite the physical and emotional distance that separated us, Aarav tried to reach out to me. He made several attempts to contact me, hoping for a chance to explain himself or perhaps mend the rift between us. However, my lingering doubts and the emotional scars of the past proved to be insurmountable barriers.

I chose to block Aarav's attempts at communication, unable to reconcile my feelings and doubts fully. The wounds from our past were still too raw, and the uncertainty about what had truly happened that day remained a heavy burden on my heart. Blocking him seemed like the only way to protect myself from the emotional turmoil that resurfaced every time he reached out.

It was a painful decision, but one that I felt was necessary for my own healing and growth. Aarav and I had once shared a close bond, but the events that had transpired had changed us irreversibly, and the distance between us seemed insurmountable. In the pursuit of our separate paths, we had become strangers to each other, forever marked by the events that had reshaped our lives.

Present Day

The persistent ring of the phone shattered the quietude of the evening, marking the intrusion of Aarav's presence into months of lingering silence. There was a brief moment of contemplation before I answered, a swirl of emotions threading through my voice.

"Hello?" I greeted, the tone caught between curiosity and a cautious wariness.

"Hey," Aarav's voice, a delicate balance of uncertainty and determination, reverberated through the line. "I've stumbled onto something big."

His cryptic proclamation piqued my interest, but the shadows of the past whispered caution. "What is it, Aarav? What did you find?"

"I can't explain over the phone. It's crucial that we meet in person," he urged, urgency tinging his words.

My reluctance lingered like an unspoken presence. "Why can't you just tell me now?"

"I promise, it's something that needs to be said face-to-face. Please, just hear me out," Aarav pleaded, a subtle desperation underscoring his words.

The plea hung in the air, and for a moment, I wavered. But the scars of the past month, the unanswered questions, and the fear of what might be revealed held me back. "I don't know, Aarav. I need time."

His voice took on a gentle but persistent cadence. "I understand, but this is important. I wouldn't ask if it wasn't. Let's meet tomorrow at the cafe near the park. Please."

There was a silence, a moment where the weight of the unspoken conversation bore down on us. "I'll think about it," I finally conceded, the resistance in my tone softening.

"Thank you," Aarav sighed with relief. "I promise, whatever it is, you deserve to know."

The call ended, leaving me with a swirl of conflicting emotions. The stubborn barricades I had erected began to crack, the plea in Aarav's voice carving a fragile opening for the possibility of understanding, closure, or perhaps, an unexpected twist in the tale.

Chapter 9

Seeds of Doubt

The shrill ring of my phone jolted me awake, the morning sun barely streaming through the blinds. I fumbled for my phone on the bedside table, squinting at the bright screen. Aarav's name flashed, and I hesitated before answering. The events of the previous evening still lingered in my mind, a tapestry of emotions woven with threads of uncertainty.

"Hello?" I answered cautiously.

"Aaditi, it's Aarav," came his voice,

I sat up, wrapping the duvet around me. "What's up?"

"Are we still on for today?" he asked, his words hanging in the air like unspoken promises.

I hesitated for a moment, contemplating the weight of his request. "Yes," I replied finally, my voice steady but laced with a newfound resolve. "But, Aarav, this will be the last time."

There was a pause on the other end as if he hadn't expected my words. When he spoke again, his voice carried a mix of regret and acceptance. "Alright, Aaditi. The last time."

As we hung up, the gravity of the decision settled in my chest. Today would mark the culmination of a journey — a journey that had twisted and turned, leaving us both changed. I couldn't deny the bittersweet taste of finality, the awareness that this chapter was drawing to a close.

I dressed in silence, the room filled with the soft rustle of fabric as I gathered my thoughts. The sun had fully emerged, casting a warm glow over the city outside. Aarav had chosen a quaint coffee shop for our meeting, a place that had witnessed the evolution of our connection.

As I stepped into the bustling cafe, the familiar scent of freshly ground coffee beans enveloped me. Aarav sat by the window, his gaze fixed on the passing world outside. Our eyes met, and for a moment, the unspoken words hung between us like delicate threads.

"This is it," he said, his tone a mixture of resignation and acceptance.

I nodded, a silent acknowledgment of the finality that hung in the air. The last chapter of our story was about to unfold, and as we sipped our coffee in that quiet corner, we both knew that whatever lay ahead would be a different narrative altogether.

Aarav's voice took on a sinister edge as he leaned in, his eyes locking onto mine with a predatory intensity.

"Aaditi, I've been doing some digging, and I found out some interesting things about Vedh. He's not who he appears to be. You need to be careful."

His words hung in the air, sending a shiver down my spine. I felt a surge of conflicting emotions — curiosity battling with apprehension. Aarav's cryptic warning about Vedh, coupled with the secrecy of his demeanor, left me on edge. Still, a part of me couldn't resist the intrigue, urging me to delve deeper into the shadows.

"What are you talking about, Aarav? Why should I believe you? And why are we discussing Vedh? I thought this was about the farewell incident."

Aarav's gaze held mine, and for a moment, the air crackled with tension. His response, however, surprised me.

"Aaditi, I understand your skepticism, but there are things you need to know. Vedh has a history, a past that's intricately woven with deceit and hidden agendas. This farewell incident is connected to him more than you realize."

My frustration boiled over, and I shot him a sharp look.

"This is absurd, Aarav! I don't have time for your conspiracy theories. We were supposed to talk about the farewell incident, not drag Vedh into this."

Aarav raised his hand, a calming gesture as he chose his words carefully.

"Aaditi, I get it. But if you want to understand what happened, you need to hear me out. Vedh isn't who you think he is, and his actions have consequences that reach beyond the surface. Let me fill in the details, and you can decide for yourself."

I looked at Aarav, uncertainty clouding my expression.

"Why are you telling me this, Aarav? Is it because you want us to get back together?"

Aarav's response came with a feigned concern, his words carefully chosen to mask any ulterior motives.

"Aaditi, I still care about you. I don't want to see you hurt. I thought you deserved to know the truth about Vedh before things got too serious between you two."

He continued, "Vedh's arrival in my life shortly before the incident can't be just a coincidence. He lived in Gurgaon at that time, and I can't help but wonder if he had a role to play in all of this."

The mention of Vedh, another person connected to that day, added yet another layer of complexity to the unfolding narrative. It was a reminder that the truth might be even more elusive than we had initially thought and that there were still many pieces of the puzzle waiting to be discovered.

My heart weighed heavily with the weight of Aarav's words. I felt torn between my feelings for Vedh and the uncertainty that Aarav's claims had brought upon me.

Aarav's voice oozed with smug satisfaction as he spoke.

"Aaditi, I've gathered screenshots, messages, and even witness accounts that prove Vedh is a lying bastard. Look for yourself."

Aarav's revelation about Vedh's communication with a girl added another layer of intrigue to the unfolding mystery. As he showed me the evidence of Instagram messages and phone calls between Vedh and this girl, my mind became a canvas absorbing the details. The content of their conversations, which hinted at a romantic relationship and the possibility of a sexual encounter, raised questions about Vedh's involvement in the events surrounding that day.

As the pieces of the puzzle fell into place, it was clear that the truth was more complex and elusive than we had ever imagined. The possibility that someone other than Aarav was involved had become a distinct possibility, and the questions that had plagued me for so long were inching closer to answers.

It was a moment of reckoning, a point at which I had to confront the possibility that my doubts about Aarav may have been misplaced. The journey to uncover the truth was far from over, but with each revelation, it became increasingly evident that Vedh's involvement could hold the key to understanding the events of that fateful day.

My hands trembled as I scrolled through the messages, my eyes widening at the supposed evidence presented by Aarav. Doubt once again crept into my heart.

"Aarav, I don't know what to think anymore. These messages... They seem so real. But I need to hear Vedh's side of the story."

Aarav responded slyly, his words dripping with insinuation.

"Aaditi, why would he ever tell you the truth? He's been playing you this entire time. You deserve someone better, someone like me who will always be honest with you."

My mind swirled with confusion. I felt torn between the supposed evidence presented by Aarav and the memories of the love and trust I shared with Vedh. Deep down, I knew that the only way to find the truth was to confront Vedh directly.

"Aarav, thank you for showing me this. But I need to hear Vedh's side of the story. I won't make any hasty decisions without talking to him first."

Aarav, feigning concern, offered a parting warning.

"Aaditi, be careful. You're just setting yourself up for more heartache. But if that's what you want, then go ahead. You'll see that I'm telling you the truth."

Filled with determination, I decided to drive to Vedh's place. It was Sunday, a day he typically preferred to indulge in a leisurely afternoon nap. The road stretched ahead, each passing mile heightening the anticipation that built within me. I couldn't shake the feeling that this journey held the potential to unravel the intricacies of the mysterious situation.

As I navigated through, the sun cast a warm glow, creating a contrast to the growing unease in my chest. Vedh's home, a place that had once been a haven of comfort, now felt like the epicenter of a storm.

Arriving at his doorstep, I took a deep breath. I had an extra key to his flat. My hand hesitated before opening the door... The air felt heavy with unspoken truths, and I steeled myself for the conversation that awaited.

The door creaked open quietly as I stepped into Vedh's home. The muted sunlight filtered through the curtains, casting a gentle glow on the room. I tiptoed toward his bedroom, my heart pounding with a mix of nerves and confusion. Vedh lay peacefully asleep, his features softened in the afternoon light.

I approached the bed, a small smile playing on my lips as I watched him, the rhythmic rise and fall of his chest a comforting sight. As I gently whispered his name, Vedh stirred, slowly opening his eyes. The surprise in his gaze turned into a radiant smile as he realized I was standing there.

"Hey, you," he murmured, his voice laced with the warmth of waking from a pleasant dream.

His arms reached out, pulling me into an embrace that felt like a dream itself. Vedh's touch was tender, and in that moment, the worries and uncertainties of the outside world seemed to fade away. He kissed me, each touch a reassurance that we were right where we belonged. As he held me close, Vedh's sleepy eyes sparkled with happiness.

Gently pulling away from Vedh's embrace, I looked into his eyes and smiled.

"Hey, love, could you freshen up a bit? There's something important I'd like to discuss," I said with a tone of earnestness.

Vedh nodded, a curious expression on his face, still basking in the warmth of our unexpected reunion. He got up from the bed, stretching out the drowsiness that clung to him. As he made his way to the bathroom, I took a moment to collect my thoughts, knowing that the conversation ahead had the potential to reshape the course of our relationship.

As Vedh emerged from the bathroom, the scent of coffee filled the air. He gave me a questioning look, the curiosity evident in his eyes.

"Hey, what brings you here? I thought you were going out with your dad," he said, a hint of confusion in his voice.

I took a deep breath, my heart heavy with the weight of what I was about to share. We sat down, the fragrant coffee cups cradled in our hands, and I began to speak.

"Well, it's about Aarav," I said, my voice carrying a mix of sadness and resolve. "I met him before coming here, and he had something to show me."

With a heavy heart, I retrieved my phone and began to show Vedh the messages, calls, and conversations Aarav had shared during our meeting. The air in the room shifted, becoming charged with tension as Vedh's eyes scanned the screen.

"I don't know how to say this, Vedh, but he claims there's more to the story. More to you," I confessed, my gaze dropping to the coffee cup in my hands.

The room fell into a heavy silence as Vedh processed the information. The aroma of coffee seemed to intensify, a bitter reminder of the bitter truth unfolding between us. The vulnerability in his eyes mirrored the ache in my heart, and for a moment, the weight of unspoken words hung in the air.

Softly, Vedh spoke, his voice carrying the weight of understanding, "Aaditi, I never meant to hurt you. There are things you need to know."

As the conversation unfolded, emotions poured out like spilled coffee, staining the canvas of our relationship. The confrontation was soft yet broken, a delicate dance of words that laid bare the complexities of love, trust, and the painful pursuit of truth.

Vedh's eyes reflected a mixture of regret and sincerity as he began to share his side of the story.

"Aaditi, I need you to listen to me," he started, his words measured. "There's a girl who approached me for a fling. But by then, I had already met you, and I didn't want to start over. I rejected her advances, but she didn't take it well."

He handed me his phone, and as I scrolled through the actual conversation, Vedh's reluctance to engage in anything beyond friendship with the girl became evident. The screenshots showed her persistence, attempting to lure him with suggestive messages and even sending explicit photos.

"I didn't want to burden you with this, Aaditi. I thought it would only hurt you," Vedh continued, his eyes earnest. "She found out about my company address and came to meet me as well. She was so sure behind me. I agreed to meet her once, but then she did not show up."

A knot tightened in my stomach as Vedh revealed the extent to which this girl had gone to create a false narrative. The weight of the situation pressed upon us, the room filled with the tension of unspoken truths. Vedh's vulnerability in sharing this unsettling chapter of his life laid bare the lengths he had gone to protect me from unnecessary pain.

Vedh's eyes held a mix of regret and sincerity as he unfolded more details of the perplexing situation.

"Aaditi, I need you to understand the full picture," he began, his words deliberate. "This girl was persistent, almost obsessive. I agreed to meet her once, and she did show up at my company. It was unsettling, to say the least."

He continued, "During our meeting, she fell sick unexpectedly. Concerned for her well-being, I offered to drop her off at her place. The images you've seen of me embracing her are not what they seem. I was merely helping her get home safely, which is why I had to carry her in my arms."

As Vedh painted a clearer picture, a sense of relief washed over me. The revelation unraveled the deceptive narrative crafted by Aarav, and Vedh's explanation added depth to the circumstances that led to those misleading images.

Confusion settled in the air as Vedh's revelation unfolded. Unsure of how to process the tangled web of information, I turned to him with a furrowed brow.

"Vedh, can you tell me where she first reached out to you?" I asked, my curiosity mingling with a sense of urgency.

Vedh calmly showed me the origin of their interaction - Instagram. As I scrolled through the messages, it became evident that this girl had initiated contact, introducing an entirely new layer to the unfolding drama.

The notifications revealed a series of messages that started innocuously but took a turn for the unexpected. The girl's persistence was palpable, and I couldn't help but wonder about the motivations behind her relentless pursuit. Vedh's responses remained consistent with his story—a polite but firm rejection of her advances.

As I scrolled through Ria's Instagram profile, the simplicity of her name, innocuous at first glance, became the epicenter of a seismic revelation. A chill ran down my spine as I clicked on her lone profile picture. The image materialized before me, and the shock was palpable—it was unmistakably Naina, my classmate.

Panic set in, an unbidden surge of adrenaline coursing through my veins. My fingers moved almost frantically, scrolling through the limited posts, each revelation intensifying the whirlwind of emotions within me. The digital and real worlds collided in a disorienting dance, and the implications of this revelation unfolded like chapters in an unexpected thriller.

The shock of discovering Naina's active profile left me breathless, my mind a labyrinth of confusion. I turned to Vedh, my eyes wide with disbelief.

"Vedh, you need to see this. Ria's Instagram has all of Naina's photos. But she's gone, Vedh. I attended her funeral. How can this be?"

Vedh's eyes widened in disbelief, uncertainty flickering across his face. "Aaditi, that's impossible. I've met her, and she's alive. Her name is Ria. Look at the profile. It's not Naina."

I scrutinized the screen, the images casting an eerie sense of déjà vu. Vedh's claim clashed with the evidence before us. The digital and the tangible collided, creating a dissonance that echoed in the room.

"How is this possible, Vedh? Naina's gone. I saw her family grieve. But if Ria is alive, then who—" I trailed off, the unspoken question lingering in the air, a riddle that demanded to unravel. The truth seemed to dance on the precipice of understanding, just out of reach, as the mystery of Naina—or Ria—deepened.

Vedh's expression shifted, a mixture of surprise and correction. "No, Aaditi, she's not dead. I met her once."

The revelation added another layer of complexity to the unfolding narrative, a twist that transformed the story into a psychological thriller. The lines between reality and illusion blurred as Vedh's words clashed with the memories etched in my mind.

"How is that possible? I attended her funeral, Vedh. I saw her family grieving," I insisted, my voice trembling with confusion.

Vedh's response held an air of mystery, "Aaditi, there's more to this than you know. I met her after the funeral. Things aren't as they seem."

The room felt like a scene from a psychological thriller, the weight of conflicting realities pressing down on us. My mind raced, attempting to reconcile the certainty of Naina's demise with the undeniable proof of her digital existence.

"Vedh, you're not making any sense. How can she be alive?" I demanded, the unraveling mystery intensifying the suspense of our conversation.

Vedh, choosing his words carefully, spoke in a hushed tone, "Aaditi, there are secrets; there is more to this story that goes beyond what we perceive. Trust me, I'm as perplexed as you are."

The conversation hung in the air, a dense fog of uncertainty enveloping us. The web of confusion tightened, leaving us entangled in the enigma of Naina's seemingly contradictory existence—a digital ghost resurrected in the wake of her perceived demise.

As the weight of the mysterious revelation lingered, I felt compelled to share the farewell story with Vedh—a tale laden with the echoes of broken trust and aching memories.

"Vedh," I began, my voice tinged with the weight of the past, "it all started at the farewell party. Aarav's behavior became increasingly erratic, and I was caught in a web of lies and deceit. He claimed an emergency, but as the night unfolded, I discovered he was concealing something."

I recounted the details—the furtive glances, the whispered conversations, and the unsettling feeling that something was amiss. The farewell, meant to be a celebration, had morphed into a haunting relationship unraveling. Aarav's actions that night were a catalyst, prompting me to part ways with him in search of clarity and honesty.

Vedh listened attentively, his eyes reflecting understanding. The room seemed to hold the weight of the past, the air thick with unspoken emotions.

With the tale laid bare, a surge of determination filled me. I needed answers. I needed to confront Aarav.

Considering the gravity of the situation, I turned to Vedh and suggested, "Before we proceed, Vedh, I think we should call Aarav. It's only fair that he hears this directly from us. We need answers, and confronting him together might illuminate the situation."

Vedh nodded in agreement, recognizing the importance of transparency in this intricate web of revelations. The decision to call Aarav became a pivotal moment, a prelude to the impending meeting with Naina. The air crackled with tension as we prepared to untangle the threads of deception that had woven their way into our lives.

I hesitated momentarily, my finger hovering over the phone's screen. The journey to unravel the mysteries of the farewell incident had taken an unexpected turn, and I was now poised at the threshold of a conversation that held the promise of answers and closure.

Aarav's voice came through the phone, curious and concerned, "Aaditi, have you seen the truth I showed you? What do you think?"

I took a deep breath, urgency pulsating through my veins, "Aarav, we need to talk in person. I'm sending you a location. Get here as soon as possible."

There was a brief pause on the other end of the line, a moment pregnant with anticipation. Aarav hesitated before finally agreeing, "Alright, I'll be there. But Aaditi, we need to clear things up."

The call ended, leaving a trail of unanswered questions and a sense of impending confrontation. The coordinates had been shared, setting the stage for a meeting that would either bring clarity or plunge us deeper into the labyrinth of secrets.

The wait for Aarav felt like an eternity, the air charged with tension as we anticipated the confrontation that awaited us. Finally, as Aarav entered the house, his eyes met Vedh's with a mixture of suspicion and accusation.

"I knew this guy was not innocent," Aarav spat, his words cutting through the room. "Come, Aaditi, we'll get you home."

I stepped forward, intercepting his impulsive move, "Aarav, let's sit down and talk first."

Reluctantly, Aarav took a seat, his eyes fixed on me with a mixture of concern and frustration. The atmosphere was charged, the silence pregnant with the weight of unspoken truths.

"Naina is alive, Aarav," I stated, watching his reaction carefully.

Aarav feigned shock, but a flicker in his eyes betrayed a different truth. Deep down, he knew that the revelation wasn't as surprising as he wanted it to be. The room became a battlefield of emotions, where the lines between ally and adversary blurred, and the quest for the truth intensified.

I took a deep breath, the weight of the situation pressing on my chest, as I explained the content Aarav had shown me. The messages, the screenshots, the videos—it was a carefully orchestrated narrative designed to cast doubt on Vedh's integrity. Aarav, seemingly caught off guard by my revelation, shifted uncomfortably in his seat.

"Who shared these messages with you, Aarav?" I asked, my voice steady but laced with urgency.

Aarav hesitated for a moment before admitting, "I received an anonymous mail, stating 'Save Aaditi from Vedh.' It contained all the photos, videos, and screenshots of the chats."

The revelation hung in the air, a clandestine force manipulating the strings of our lives. The conversation took an unexpected turn, transforming into a strategic discussion about the enigmatic figure orchestrating the shadows—someone with a vested interest in disrupting the course of our relationships.

Vedh, sensing the need for a united front, spoke with determination, "We can't let this manipulation tear us apart. Let's plan and take hold of Naina. Together, we can uncover the truth and expose the puppet master pulling the strings."

The room became a war room of sorts, a space where alliances were formed against a common adversary. The decision to confront Naina took root in the shared determination to unravel the intricacies of the elaborate charade that threatened to engulf us all.

Vedh: Hey Ria! Missed our talks. How about we spice things up this weekend?

Ria: Oh, Vedh! I was hoping you'd say that. Spill the details. 😉

Vedh: How about at my place? I've got a few tricks up my sleeve.

Ria: (winking emoji) Your place, huh? What's the plan, naughty boy?

Vedh: Oh, you'll love this. I've got a little interrogation scenario in mind. Something thrilling.

Aarav and I couldn't help but exchange amused glances as we sneakily read Vedh's scandalous conversation.

Ria: Interrogation, you say? Now, you've piqued my interest. What's in it for me?

Vedh:(smirking emoji) Well, let's just say it involves getting to know each other on a whole new level. Ready for some excitement?

As Vedh continued his playful conversation, the exchange took a decidedly flirtatious turn, with the promise of an adventure that went far beyond the ordinary catch-up.

Ria: (devilish emoji) Excitement is my middle name. Spill the juicy details, Vedh.

Vedh: (winking emoji) How about a little love-making interrogation? 😉

Ria: (blushing emoji) You're naughty, Vedh. Can't wait for the weekend!

The digital dialogue crackled with electrifying energy, leaving no doubt that the upcoming weekend would be a spicy adventure – where desires would simmer, and secrets might just burst into flames.

Chapter 10

Whispers of the Unseen

As the weekend approached, Vedh's apartment transformed into a clandestine stage for an enigmatic encounter. What Vedh didn't know was that Ria was merely a pseudonym, concealing the true identity of the mysterious woman known as Naina. The playful banter that had unfolded in their messages masked a deeper game, one that Vedh was about to unwittingly enter.

When Naina, the woman behind Ria's carefully crafted persona, arrived at Vedh's apartment, the atmosphere was thick with suspense. Vedh, playing his part with a disarming smile, guided her into a dimly lit living room. Unbeknownst to her, Aarav and I hid in the shadows of separate rooms, silently observing the unfolding drama.

As the evening progressed, Vedh, with a sudden and unexpected intensity, took a bold turn. Subtle flirtation transformed into a calculated move as he, with a swift and unforeseen maneuver, secured Naina to the bedroom.

Aarav and I, emerging from our hidden positions, entered Vedh's bedroom. The dim light cast eerie shadows on the walls, creating a surreal ambiance that mirrored the mysterious turn of events.

Vedh whispered, "The game has changed, Ria. It's time for the real interrogation."

Her eyes widened with a mix of surprise and uncertainty as the room seemed to close in on her. The questions that followed weren't the playful inquiries from their earlier messages. Instead, they delved into the shadows of her past, probing for the truth that lay buried beneath the facade. Ria, bound to the bed, struggled to maintain composure, her mysterious aura slowly unraveling in the face of the relentless questioning.

The room was shrouded in a hushed tension as Vedh, Aarav, and I faced Ria, who lay bound to the bed. The playful facade had crumbled, revealing a woman caught in the web of her own deception.

"Ria, or whoever you are, it's time for the truth. Who are you really?" Vedh's voice held a firm determination, demanding answers.

Ria's gaze faltered for a moment, her mysterious allure now replaced by a flicker of vulnerability.

"Your real name is Naina. Why weave this intricate web of deception?" Aarav confronted her with a blunt question, cutting through the layers of illusion.

The shadows seemed to dance on the walls, mirroring the complex layers of the enigma they were attempting to unravel. Ria, bound and exposed, hesitated before her words tumbled out.

"What shadows are you hiding from, Naina? There's more to this than meets the eye," I added, my inquiry joining the relentless pursuit of truth.

"Your game is up. What's the real purpose behind this elaborate charade?" Vedh pressed, intensifying the scrutiny.

"What are you really after, Naina? The truth—no more games," Aarav demanded, his tone unwavering.

The questions, now more pointed and demanding, echoed through the room, creating an atmosphere that mirrored the intensity of a thriller. Ria, compelled to lay bare the fragments of her enigmatic past, struggled against the confines of her own secrets.

"I attended your funeral, Naina. Why this name, Ria? What is all this? Why did you fake your own death?" I asked, unraveling another layer of her elaborate ruse.

Her voice trembled as she began to unravel the tangled threads of her elaborate charade.

"Yes, my name is Naina. I never meant for things to spiral out of control like this," Naina confessed, her words echoing with the weight of her admission. Vedh, Aarav, and I exchanged bewildered glances, grappling with the unexpected revelations.

She continued, her words punctuated by heavy sighs and intermittent sobs. She confessed to orchestrating a meticulously planned scheme designed to sow seeds of discord and destruction. "I wanted revenge. I wanted to see Aarav's reputation crumble, and I wanted to break the bond between you two."

Her eyes, filled with remorse, met mine, acknowledging the pain she had inflicted on our relationship. Aarav's expression hardened as he absorbed the gravity of her words.

Aarav asked again, "What are you talking about? What could drive you to such lengths?"

Her tale unfolded like a dark novel, revealing how she had plotted to fake an assault on the farewell day, intending to tarnish Aarav's character and create a rift between him and me.

She replied, "I felt cornered, betrayed. I thought this was the only way to make you both suffer as much as I had."

Her confession unraveled a complex web of resentment, jealousy, and despair. The betrayal weighed heavy, casting a shadow on the friendships that had once seemed unbreakable.

I asked, "But why involve Aarav? What did he do to deserve this?"

Her eyes, red from tears, met mine. Her voice wavered as she explained the perceived injustices that fueled her misguided quest for retribution." It was a twisted logic in my head. I thought if I could make you question Aarav's trustworthiness, it would somehow make me feel less alone in my pain."

She continued, "Faking my own suicide was a risk, but I was desperate. I love Rudhay so much that I was willing to go to any length to get his love and attention."

A bombshell that shattered the remnants of trust and understanding for us. The weight of her words pressed heavily on each of us, and my heart sank at the revelation of her manipulation.

I was confused, "Rudhay?? What are you talking about? How could you involve him in this?"

In the quietude of that dimly lit room, the mere mention of Rudhay's name echoed like a thunderclap. Rudhay, the friend I had considered my confidant, sent shockwaves through the room. Vedh and Aarav exchanged bewildered glances, each struggling to comprehend the depth of Naina's misguided actions.

Aarav's expression darkened as he processed the extent of Naina's deceit. The bonds of friendship, once strong, are now strained under the weight of betrayal.

Vedh: "This is beyond revenge, Naina. You've jeopardized lives and manipulated emotions. What did you hope to achieve?"

Tears streaming down her face, she struggled to articulate the rationale behind her misguided actions.

Her confession hung in the air, each word a dark revelation that cast a shadow over us. Vedh, Aarav, and I exchanged stunned glances as the narrative took an unexpected turn.

Naina: "Rudhay's obsession for Aaditi was so intense that he orchestrated a series of events to break you guys apart."

Her words landed like a heavy blow, the implications of Rudhay's sinister motives unraveling before us. Vedh's meticulous plan to uncover the truth now expanded beyond the original scope, delving into a twisted narrative of manipulation and betrayal.

Naina continued, her voice shaky yet resolute, as she unveiled the depths of Rudhay's dark obsession." When you finally moved away from Aarav, He was ecstatic. He would have sex with me almost every day, treating me nicely. But the day he found out about Vedh, everything changed. He became harsh, and the nights turned into a nightmare. The sex became rough, and he would beat me up, claiming it was my fault that Vedh had entered the picture."

The shocking details painted a horrifying picture of Rudhay's twisted mindset, his actions fueled by jealousy and a desire for control.

"But then why target Vedh? What did he have against him?" I asked, trying to understand the motive behind Rudhay's malevolence.

Her eyes, filled with a mixture of fear and sorrow, met mine. She explained that Rudhay saw Vedh as a threat to the twisted reality he had constructed. Vedh's presence disrupted the carefully woven web of control Rudhay had over Aaditi.

"This is madness. Rudhay was manipulating you, manipulating all of us," Vedh remarked, grappling with the unsettling truth.

She nodded, the weight of her own victimhood etched across her face. The room became a battleground of emotions as the revelations unraveled a web of deceit and abuse.

Aarav, his disbelief transforming into anger, stood up, confronting the harsh truth that someone he considered a friend had perpetrated such cruelty. "We need to expose Rudhay for who he really is," he declared with conviction.

Vedh, Aarav, and I grappled with the disturbing truth that Rudhay, the person we had once considered a friend, had been orchestrating a sinister plot all along.

Naina explained that Rudhay perceived Vedh as a rival, a disruptor of the twisted equilibrium he had maintained. Vedh's emergence shattered Rudhay's illusion of control, pushing him over the edge into a realm of brutality.

"This is beyond comprehension. We need to put an end to Rudhay's manipulations," Vedh insisted, determined to bring an end to the ongoing torment.

A cauldron of conflicting emotions set the stage for a confrontation that transcended the boundaries of their original plan. Aarav, once a pawn in Rudhay's scheme, now stood resolved to expose the darkness that lurked within our circle.

"We'll bring Rudhay to justice. No one deserves to endure what Naina went through," Aarav declared, his anger now channeled into a sense of responsibility.

Naina, her eyes a tumultuous sea of emotions, interjected with a mix of urgency and desperation, "No, you can't confront Rudhay directly. He's unpredictable and dangerous. He won't hesitate to retaliate."

Her plea served as a stark reminder of the immediate danger that surrounded us, now brimming with a newfound sense of urgency.

"We can't let him continue this reign of manipulation and abuse. We need a plan, something that ensures everyone's safety," Vedh asserted, his determination matching the gravity of the situation.

The room, once a space of shared secrets, transformed into a makeshift war room. Aarav, Vedh, and I exchanged determined glances, acknowledging the need for strategic action.

"We can gather evidence and expose his actions without directly confronting him. We need to protect everyone involved," I suggested, charting a course that aimed at dismantling Rudhay's facade while minimizing risks.

Aarav, his anger now channeled into a resolute determination, nodded in agreement. The room, now buzzing with a renewed sense of purpose, was focused on the collective goal.

"We need to unravel Rudhay's network of manipulation. Expose his actions, ensure he can't harm anyone else," Vedh concluded, laying the groundwork for the challenging path ahead.

The gravity of the situation stretched the very fabric of our friendship, resulting in a tense atmosphere fraught with unspoken questions. How had Rudhay, the person we'd entrusted with our hearts, become the puppeteer orchestrating this intricate web of deception? Vedh's brow furrowed, and Aarav's eyes widened, each of us struggling to reconcile the friend we thought we knew with the puppet master who now lurked in the shadows. The revelation of his toxic influences cast a pall over the room, and the intimate details she shared about Rudhay's hold over her sent shivers down our spines.

In the shadowy corners of their shared secrets, Naina confessed, her voice weighed down by the chains of an unbearable truth. “No, he has a strong grip on me. He possesses my videos and threatens to expose me whenever I try to break free.”

The revelation hung heavy in the air, casting a pall of collective helplessness over the group. The gravity of Rudhay’s manipulation extended far beyond what any of them had anticipated, leaving them simmering in a cauldron of despair.

As the unsettling truth settled in, I spoke out, my determination cutting through the stifling silence. “This is beyond unacceptable. We can’t let him continue this exploitation. We need to find a way to put an end to it.”

Aarav’s expression hardened, absorbing the shock of Naina’s words. Vedh, visibly disturbed yet resolute, pledged to bring Rudhay to justice.

Vedh declared, his voice carrying the weight of determination, “We’ll expose him for the monster he is. We need a plan to ensure Naina’s safety and to bring down Rudhay’s web of manipulation.”

In a moment of heartbreaking disclosure, Naina shared a dark chapter of Rudhay’s obsession. “You don’t know this, but Rudhay’s fixation on Aaditi dates back to our teenage years. He would stalk her, observing her closely and even resorting to unspeakable acts during annual gatherings.” The shadows of the past began to intertwine with the urgency of the present, creating a tapestry of secrets and betrayal that demanded unraveling.

A collective gasp swept through the room as the revelation sank in. The once familiar image of Rudhay, their supposed friend, now morphed into something darker, something far more sinister.

As the unsettling truth unfolded, I couldn't help but voice the shared sentiment, my words heavy with the weight of realization. "This is beyond disturbing. How could we have been so blind to his actions?"

Aarav, visibly seething with anger, clenched his fists, grappling with the shock of our collective naivety. Vedh's expression mirrored a mix of disbelief and disgust, urging Naina to reveal more details as if peeling back the layers of Rudhay's twisted obsession.

Naina, burdened by the weight of her confession, spoke of the dark depths of Rudhay's fixation. "He would attend Aaditi's performances during annual gatherings, lurking in the shadows, where he would masturbate while watching her. His obsession escalated, and he would often imagine me as Aaditi during our encounters." The chilling revelation unraveled a narrative of perversion and deceit that had long been hidden in the shadows.

As the group grappled with the shocking revelations, a sense of urgency permeated the room. The plan to dismantle Rudhay's manipulation had taken on a new dimension—a mission not only to free Naina but also to protect Aaditi from the depths of Rudhay's dark obsession.

Naina revealed the orchestrated web of deceit spun by Rudhay. "He sent me here and manipulated me into seducing

Vedh, all while gathering videos of our encounters. His plan was to send them anonymously to Aarav, creating chaos between Aaditi and Vedh and ultimately forcing Aaditi out of their lives."

Aarav's eyes burned with anger, and my own disbelief mirrored the shock that rippled through the group.

I exclaimed, my voice reflecting incredulity, "He used you as a pawn in his sick game to manipulate all of us?"

Naina nodded, her gaze fixed on the ground as if unable to meet our eyes. The revelation peeled back another layer of Rudhay's malevolence, exposing the extent of his calculated cruelty.

Aarav, his voice seething with anger, demanded answers. "Why? What did he gain from tearing us apart?"

Naina explained, her voice tinged with sorrow, "He wanted Aaditi out of your life. He believed that without her, Vedh would be vulnerable, and he could control every aspect of our lives. He just wants Aaditi to be lonely so that she can finally be with him."

Vedh, his fists clenched, struggled to process the magnitude of Rudhay's deceit.

"This is beyond obsession. It's a sick game of control. We need to expose him, put an end to this madness, and keep Aaditi safe as well," Vedh declared with determination.

Concerned about Naina's immediate safety, I inquired, "Where are you staying, Naina? How did he let you come here?"

Naina, her eyes reflecting a mix of fear and despair, disclosed the chilling details. "He asked me to get a video, and he's waiting for me downstairs in the car."

The tension in the air thickened, the weight of the impending confrontation with Rudhay casting a shadow over the group.

Vedh, his jaw set with determination, spoke urgently. "We need to act fast. Let's get her to safety and expose Rudhay before he can execute the next phase of his plan."

Aarav, fueled by a mix of anger and concern, agreed. The group rallied together, driven by a shared determination to unravel Rudhay's malicious machinations and protect those he sought to harm.

"We can't let him continue manipulating us. Naina, do you have a plan? How can we ensure your safety?" Aarav's voice resonated with urgency and concern.

Her eyes darting nervously, Naina revealed a plan to rendezvous with Rudhay in the car and create a distraction, allowing the group to intervene and extricate her from the situation.

"I'll signal you when I'm in the car. That's when you can approach and expose him for what he is," Naina explained.

"Let's not rush into this, Naina. We'll call our gang, gather more support, and confront Rudhay together. Safety comes first," I suggested.

Vedh and Aarav nodded in agreement, recognizing the need for a well-coordinated approach to dismantle Rudhay's manipulative scheme.

"We'll make sure you're not alone in this. Once our gang is here, we'll expose Rudhay for everything he's done," Vedh affirmed.

"He won't get away with this. We'll put an end to his games tonight," Aarav declared, fueled by a mix of anger and determination.

Though visibly relieved at the prospect of additional support, Naina still harbored a sense of urgency.

"But what if he gets suspicious? I don't want him to do something drastic before you all arrive," she voiced her concern.

A thoughtful pause filled the room before Aarav spoke. "We'll play it smart. We won't let him suspect anything until we're ready. The element of surprise is on our side."

"Alright, we need to coordinate this carefully. Naina, once you're in the car, give us a signal. We'll approach discreetly and catch him off guard," Vedh outlined the plan.

Naina, her nerves evident, nodded in agreement. The weight of the impending confrontation seemed to hang heavily in the air.

"We'll have a couple of members stationed nearby to ensure nothing goes wrong. The rest of us will be ready to step in when needed," I added.

"Let's make sure he doesn't have an inkling of what's about to hit him," Aarav emphasized.

"Remember, the goal is to expose him without putting anyone at risk. We'll be there for you, Naina," Vedh reassured.

Naina, though anxious, seemed bolstered by the support around her. "I'm ready. Let's put an end to this."

Sarah and Monish found themselves coincidentally hanging out together when my urgent call interrupted their day. I quickly briefed Sarah about the shocking scenario unfolding, and the gravity of the situation resonated with her as well. Without hesitation, they decided to join us in the plan.

As they made their way toward us, I explained every detail over the call, ensuring they were brought up to speed with the unfolding events. The urgency in their voices mirrored the tense atmosphere that had gripped the group.

Sarah: "We're on our way. Just tell us where to meet you."

The proximity of their location allowed them to reach us in just 20 minutes, a brief yet crucial window of time that would play a pivotal role in the unfolding confrontation with Rudhay. The decision for Sarah and Monish to join us not only bolstered our numbers but also added valuable support and expertise to the group.

"Guys, once we expose Rudhay, we need to involve the authorities. We can't let him escape the legal consequences of his actions." I asserted, emphasizing the importance of holding Rudhay accountable.

Sarah and Monish, fully aware of the gravity of the situation, quickly agreed.

"We'll be ready to provide the necessary support and ensure everything is documented for legal proceedings." Sarah assured.

Monish added his commitment, "And if Rudhay tries anything, we won't hesitate to step in. We need to make sure everyone stays safe."

With the roles clearly defined, the gang dispersed to their assigned positions, preparing for the pivotal moment when Rudhay's manipulative games would be laid bare.

As the minutes ticked away, the room buzzed with a sense of anticipation. The gang members, communicating through discreet signals and messages, prepared for the impending confrontation. Each member stood poised, ready to act when the signal came, united in their resolve to expose Rudhay and ensure justice prevailed.

Chapter 11
Untangling The Threads

Rudhay's Perspective

From the moment I first laid eyes on Aaditi, an inexplicable connection forged within me. We shared the same locality, attended the same tuition center, and were friends, yet mere friendship felt inadequate. I yearned for more, for her.

I couldn't comprehend why Aaditi didn't see me the way I saw her. I believed I was the protagonist of my own story, and everything should align with my desires. Aaditi's lack of romantic interest became a challenge, a conquest that fueled my determination. I thought, "How could she resist someone like me?"

As a teenager, my feelings for Aaditi went beyond friendship. She was like a puzzle, and I was determined to solve it, to claim her as my own. In my mind, I deserved her affection and admiration. It wasn't a matter of if but when. The world, in my eyes, was mine for the taking.

When Aaditi's mother passed away, I became her pillar of support. I was there when she needed someone to lean on, offering a comforting presence that seemed to ease her pain.

As the tears flowed, so did the bond between us. Her touch, once innocent and consoling, began to ignite an unfamiliar fire within me.

Time marched on, and Aaditi's life took a turn that I hadn't anticipated. Aarav entered the scene, and gradually, he became the new chapter in her life. I, however, couldn't bear to witness the person I cared about finding peace in the arms of another. As she and Aarav's relationship blossomed, my world crumbled.

The pain of unrequited love morphed into a relentless obsession. The very thought of her with someone else, particularly Aarav, sparked a firestorm of jealousy within me. My emotions, once a tumultuous sea beneath a calm surface, now churned violently. I felt myself losing control, slipping into darkness fueled by my all-consuming desire for Aaditi.

My joy knew no bounds when Aaditi had a series of arguments with Aarav. Well, Aarav is an egoistic bastard. The only opinion that he seemed to care about is his own. She and Aarav had a bitter fight when she saw a series of 'hot' and 'spicy' messages from a girl Aarav had received, and most of the time, Aarav did take her for granted.

She felt cheated, and all of her close friends, including myself, began comforting her. Aarav was a rich brat who had everything... I saw it as an opportunity.

That evening, I messaged Aaditi and asked her to meet me at the coffee shop outside our college. When I reached the coffee shop, She was already there. She had ordered my favorite latte.

I nervously approached Aaditi at the coffee shop. She looked up, her eyes still carrying the weight of recent heartbreak.

I approached Aaditi with a smile, my heart pounding with a mix of nervousness and anticipation.

"Hey, Aaditi. Would you mind if I join you for a moment?" I asked, hoping my attempt at casualness wasn't too transparent.

"Oh, Rudhay! Sure, take a seat," Aaditi responded, welcoming me to join her.

Taking a deep breath, I prepared to broach the delicate subject that had been weighing on my mind.

"I heard about what happened with Aarav. I'm really sorry that you're going through this," I said, trying to convey genuine sympathy.

"Yeah, it's been tough. But I'll get through it," Aaditi sighed, her vulnerability palpable.

I shifted the conversation, gathering my courage to express my deeper feelings.

"Aaditi, I've been meaning to talk to you about us. I've always cared about you, and I hate seeing you hurt like this," I confessed, my heart racing.

Aaditi looked at me, a mix of curiosity and exhaustion in her eyes. "What do you mean, Rudhay?" she inquired, and I knew it was time to lay my cards on the table.

"I mean... I've always felt a deep connection with you. I love you, Aaditi. I want to be there for you, to make you happy," I nervously revealed, hoping my feelings were reciprocated.

Aaditi responded softly, expressing her need for space after the recent events with Aarav.

"Rudhay, you're a great friend. But after what happened with Aarav, I need some time alone. I hope you understand," she explained kindly, and my disappointment was palpable.

I nodded, acknowledging her feelings. "I get that, Aaditi. But I can't help how I feel. I want to be more than just a friend to you."

Aaditi, maintaining her kind demeanor, clarified her stance, "Rudhay, you've always been like a brother to me. I appreciate your feelings, but I don't see you in that way. I need someone who can give me space right now."

Understanding her perspective, I nodded, saying, "I understand, Aaditi. I just wanted you to know how I feel."

She smiled and thanked me for my honesty, suggesting, "Let's just focus on being friends for now, okay?"

Returning the smile, I agreed, "Yeah, of course. Friends it is," masking the disappointment and hoping that time might change her feelings.

As we continued our conversation, the both of us delved into various topics, attempting to move past the moment of emotional vulnerability. The coffee shop ambiance provided a soothing backdrop, with the aroma of freshly brewed coffee lingering in the air.

Rudhay, attempting to shift the focus away from the intense emotions swirling between them, changed the subject.

"So, how have you been coping with everything, Aaditi? Have you talked to anyone about it?" I asked, hoping to provide a momentary respite.

She was sipping her coffee and shared, "Yeah, I've been talking to my close friends. It helps, you know? Sharing your feelings with someone who understands."

"That's good to hear. I'm here for you too, as a friend, if you ever need someone to talk to," I offered, trying to convey a sense of support.

Aaditi, smiling appreciatively, responded, "Thanks, Rudhay. I appreciate that. Friends like you make it a bit easier."

Nodding, I acknowledged, "I'm glad I can be there for you in whatever way you need."

Aaditi, sensing the need for a lighter atmosphere, decided to change the topic.

"So, how's everything with you? Anything new happening in your life?" she inquired, steering the conversation toward a more casual terrain.

Grinning, I shared a personal development. "Not much, just the usual work stuff. But you know what's new? I started taking guitar lessons. Thought it might be a good way to relax."

Intrigued, She responded, "That's awesome! I didn't know you were into music. How's it going?"

With enthusiasm, I shared, "It's challenging, but I enjoy it. Maybe someday I'll play a song for you."

Aaditi, smiling, replied, "I'd like that. It sounds like a great way to unwind," creating a momentary diversion from the heavier topics that lingered beneath the surface.

Approximately 30 minutes later, Aaditi and I parted ways. She smiled at me and thanked me for being by her side at this hour of need. Soon enough

This conversation formed a significant part of my life. I realized that nobody loved me. I also realized that she had friend-zoned me because I wasn't good enough.

I always felt like I blended into the background, just an ordinary guy in the same locality as Aaditi. No flashy charm, no extraordinary talents – just an average teenager trying to make sense of the world. And perhaps that was my downfall.

I couldn't help but think that Aaditi never saw me as anything more than a friend because I didn't stand out. In a world where everyone seemed to be striving for attention and recognition, I was content with being low-key. But as I developed feelings for Aaditi, I couldn't shake the thought that maybe my ordinariness was the reason she didn't like me romantically.

She was surrounded by people who exuded confidence and uniqueness, traits that seemed to be light-years away from my own. I'd watch as others caught her attention effortlessly, leaving me on the sidelines, just another face in the crowd. It made me question if I was simply too ordinary to be noticed, especially in a romantic sense.

I've become increasingly self-conscious about my appearance and personality, wondering if I needed to transform into someone more captivating to catch her eye. Maybe, I thought, if I stood out more, she would finally see me in a different light.

My dad owned a media business. I had a bright future in front of my very eyes, but my eyes wanted to see Aaditi since she was the apple of my eye.

As I delved into my internship at my father's media company, I found myself engrossed in the dynamic world of journalism. Naina, an intern assigned to cover the beauty and lifestyle segment, was a familiar face in the office. Little did I know, we were not only colleagues but also classmates, sharing the same educational journey. She was a young and charming girl. Her ideas were fresh and unique. I knew she had a crush on me.

Caught up in the whirlwind of media tasks and responsibilities, I failed to realize our connection until a casual encounter in the office cafeteria brought it to light.

In the bustling atmosphere of the media office, I found myself casually approaching Naina, a familiar face from the beauty section.

"Hey, Naina, right? I see you quite often, especially in the beauty section," I greeted her.

Naina responded with a warm smile, affirming, "Yes, that's me. I'm interning for beauty and lifestyle. How about you?"

As I shared my own internship experience, I realized our paths crossed not only in the workplace but possibly in the academic realm as well.

"By the way, do we happen to study in the same class?" Naina asked, piquing my curiosity.

Surprised, I admitted, "Wait, really? I had no idea. I guess we've been too absorbed in our work to notice."

We shared a laugh, acknowledging the common tendency to be engrossed in our respective responsibilities. In the midst of this revelation, Naina posed a thoughtful question.

"So, what are your thoughts on the internship so far?" she inquired.

Reflecting on the challenges and the valuable insights gained in the dynamic media industry, I responded, "It's been quite a challenge, but I'm learning a ton about the media industry."

In the following days, Naina and I found common ground, exchanging insights about our studies and experiences in the media house and even collaborating on some projects. What started as an oversight became an opportunity to cultivate a friendship beyond our assigned tasks, enriching my internship experience and broadening my perspective within the professional realm.

One evening, after a casual dinner and some shared laughter, the atmosphere between us shifted. The connection we had developed sparked an intimate moment, leading to a level of closeness we hadn't explored before. It was a new chapter in our friendship, one that added a layer of complexity to our relationship.

Naina and I couldn't help it. I kissed her, and she obliged. Soon enough, we were busy undressing each other. I knew she wanted me. I unbuttoned her shirt and began kissing her breasts. She did not resist because she knew I could help her, both personally and professionally. I removed her bra and slid my hand in her denim. Her underwear was all wet. I think she was expecting it. I took her to my car, and we made love.

I ate her pussy like a child who's hungry for food. It was the first time that I had deflowered a woman. Naina was an innocent soul, and she loved me, but I loved Aaditi (and nobody else). Naina was just a way I had found in order to fulfill my wicked sexual desires.

After a shared intimate moment, Naina opened up to me about a dream that had been brewing in her mind – to kickstart her own media website, one that would showcase 'unbiased' news.

Naina, brimming with excitement, exclaimed, "I've been thinking a lot, and I want to start my own media/news website. Something that reflects my vision and values."

Supportively, I responded, "That sounds amazing, Naina! What's your vision for it?"

As Naina passionately unfolded her plans, detailing themes, content strategy, and the unique perspective she wished to bring to the media landscape, her enthusiasm became contagious, sparking my own excitement for her ambitious venture.

"Enthusiastically, I chimed in, "I love the idea, Naina! How can I support you in making this dream a reality?"

Grateful for my support, Naina expressed, "I knew you'd be on board! Your support means a lot to me. Let's work on this together."

I found myself luring Naina into the web of my desires. She had once confessed her feelings for me, and now, in a twisted turn of events, I exploited that vulnerability. Naina willingly embraced the role of my submissive, her happiness evident in her eager agreement.

However, my desires remained fixated on Aaditi. Naina, though a willing participant in this intricate dance, was merely a pawn in the complex game that unfolded in the recesses of my mind. She became a temporary distraction, a means to satisfy a void that Aaditi's absence had carved within me.

The lines between manipulation and genuine connection blurred as I navigated this twisted path. Naina's affection and compliance became a facade, a cover for the obsession that continued to tighten its grip on my soul. The complexity of emotions threatened to overwhelm me, but the allure of having Aaditi in my life as more than just a confidante fueled my actions.

On the farewell day, In a dimly lit room, I sat with Naina, our eyes reflecting the dark determination that fueled our revenge against Aarav.

I was always a master at strategizing and formulation. Therefore, constructing a plan in order to frame Aarav wasn't difficult. I, however, knew that the plan had to be flawless.

My scheme unfolded according to the following plan:

Step 1: Win Naina over by feigning affection and convincing her of my love.

Step 2: Manipulate Naina into calling Aarav urgently at the Hotel in Gurgaon, making it seem like a dire situation. To make the ruse more convincing, I resorted to physical violence, deliberately leaving bruises on Naina's face.

Step 3: Naina was tasked with seducing Aarav and engaging in a sexual encounter. The aftermath of this act was crucial, as traces of Aarav's semen would be strategically left on the bedsheet and Naina's body.

Step 4: To further incapacitate Aarav, I added sleeping pills to his drink at the hotel, ensuring he would succumb to drowsiness and "go to sleep" as part of the plan.

"So, Naina, this plan needs to be flawless. Aarav has to believe he's genuinely helping in an emergency," I whispered, my voice laden with vindictiveness.

Naina, her mischievous eyes matching mine, nodded. "Don't worry, Rudhay. He'll be here, unsuspecting, and we'll set the stage for the ultimate revelation." Aarav entered the dimly lit hotel, and my gaze met Naina's, silently affirming our readiness to proceed with the twisted plan. With a confident nod, we stepped into the room, the air heavy with a malevolence that only fueled my determination.

She had crafted a cunning excuse, a call that he couldn't refuse. She lured him in with a pretext that tugged at his emotions, ensuring he would come to meet her, unsuspecting of the twisted plot awaiting him.

Playing the charming hostess, Naina offered Aarav a drink, initiating a seductive dance that would set the stage for the dark plot we had planned. I had carefully spiked Aarav's drink, ensuring he would be lost in intoxication, oblivious to the impending betrayal.

The calculated manipulation continued as she, seemingly overwhelmed by genuine emotions, portrayed herself as a victim coerced into sex. Unbeknownst to Aarav, every moment was meticulously recorded on her phone—a potent weapon in my scheme to shatter Aaditi's trust. The room, registered under the alias Hedoy Mahanta, became the theater for a careful act of deceit.

Guiding Naina through the performance, I coached her to manipulate the scenario further. "You're doing great, Naina. Make him believe Aaditi is betraying him," I instructed, satisfaction and vengeance intertwining in my voice.

With the scripted physical encounter concluded, I retrieved the damning footage, handing it to a shadowy figure in the background—a well-paid operative tasked with unleashing controlled chaos by leaking the video on social media. "Ensure it's selective chaos," I emphasized, fully aware that the next phase of our revenge was set to unfold.

Naina and I exchanged a glance of wicked satisfaction. The meticulously executed plan had worked flawlessly, leaving a trail of devastation in its wake. Little did we realize the far-reaching consequences of the chaos we had unleashed—a web of deceit and malevolence that would scar not only Aarav but also the lives entangled in our sinister plot.

Soon enough, after Aarav's exit from Aaditi's life, a subtle sense of contentment settled within me. The opportunity to be close to Aaditi and share moments with her brought a satisfying warmth to my heart. While the desire to deepen our connection lingered,

Observing Aaditi from afar became a source of joy. Her laughter, her quirks, and the way she carried herself — each detail etched in my mind. The notion of making love to her flickered in my thoughts, but the fear of tarnishing the foundation of our friendship held me back. I yearned for the right time, a moment when the stars would align and our connection could evolve naturally.

Days turned into weeks and weeks into months, yet I bided my time, waiting for the opportune moment to approach Aaditi. Our friendship, precious and fragile, meant more to me than a fleeting romantic encounter. I envisioned a future where our connection could blossom into something deeper and more meaningful.

As the seasons changed, so did the dynamics of our interactions. I savored every shared smile and cherished the closeness that defined our friendship. The unspoken bond between us hinted at a potential for more, and I patiently waited for the right moment to express the emotions that simmered beneath the surface.

In the quiet corners of my heart, where the shadows of longing and regret lingered, I hatched a plan born from a desperate desire to keep Aaditi tethered to the echoes of our shared past. Consumed by an unyielding yearning, I began a charade that blurred the lines between truth and deception.

In the dim glow of my computer screen, I meticulously composed messages that mirrored the cadence of Aarav's voice, reviving the laughter and intimacy we once held dear. The old conversations, snippets of a time when our connection was unburdened by the weight of separation, resurfaced in her inbox. I had also sent gifts on the pretext of Aarav to make sure she felt he was sitting with her, not leaving her.

I knew the danger in what I was doing, threading the line between a yearning heart and the ethical boundaries of love. Yet, the selfish desire to ensure Aaditi never moved beyond the realm of our shared history fueled my actions. I even hired people who could stalk her and make her feel unsafe, as she was somehow scared of Aarav's actions.

After three years of quietly watching Aaditi, the delicate balance I had maintained began to unravel when I stumbled upon a revelation — Vedh. The name echoed in the corridors of my consciousness, casting a shadow over the contentment I had found in silently observing Aaditi.

Vedh, an unexpected presence in Aaditi's life, became a disruptive force in the backdrop of my carefully crafted emotions. The revelation felt like a sudden storm, shaking the foundations of the world I had built around my feelings for her. Questions swirled in my mind — who was Vedh, and how did he fit into Aaditi's life?

The realization that there was another contender for Aaditi's affections stirred a mix of emotions within me. Jealousy, perhaps, but also a profound sadness as I grappled with the potential shift in dynamics. The idea of Vedh becoming a significant part of Aaditi's world challenged the narrative I had envisioned for us.

As I stumbled upon Vedh and Aaditi locked in an intimate embrace, a tumult of emotions swept through me like a relentless storm. Jealousy, anger, and heartbreak collided within, forming a toxic concoction that threatened to obliterate any remnants of reason. My chest constricted, and the world blurred as the stark reality of the scene etched itself into my mind.

Witnessing Aaditi passionately kissing Vedh in the confines of his car, my love for her morphed into seething anger. The desire to shatter Aaditi's happiness, to be in Vedh's place, to feel what he felt, consumed me.

The sight of them together felt like an agonizing betrayal by Aaditi, the object of my long-standing affection. The emotions surged with such intensity; it went beyond mere jealousy, delving into a profound sense of inadequacy, a belief that I was somehow unworthy compared to Vedh.

In that gripping moment, a dark thought flickered across my mind – the desire to harm Vedh. An unfiltered rage pulsed through my veins, drowning rational thought. An irrational urge gripped me, compelling me to eliminate the source of my anguish, to reclaim what I deemed rightfully mine. Vedh's image with Aaditi fueled a darkness within me, an abyss I never knew existed.

The world around me faded into insignificance, leaving only the indelible image of Vedh and Aaditi together burned into my consciousness like a haunting nightmare. The agony of rejection mingled with burning jealousy, forging a toxic blend that threatened to engulf me entirely.

The emotions that coursed through me were a tumultuous blend of sadness, anger, and an acute sense of loss. I felt adrift in a sea of emotions, unable to escape the piercing waves of reality crashing upon me. Aaditi, once the beacon of my desires, now seemed like a distant star, forever out of reach.

As I grappled with the bitter truth, revenge flickered in the recesses of my wounded heart. The sting of betrayal fueled a desire for retribution against Vedh, the perceived usurper of what was once mine. Thoughts of vengeance danced on the edges of reason, a dark echo of the pain I felt.

From a distance, I watched as Aaditi's laughter echoed in the parking lot, a symphony of joy that seemed to dance effortlessly in Vedh's arms. The warmth of their embrace, the shared smiles, and the connection they exuded felt like a cruel reminder of what I once thought could be mine.

Hurt gripped me, tightening its cold fingers around my heart. It was a visceral pain, the kind that gnawed at the very core of my being. Why was she, once again, slipping away from me? The question echoed in the recesses of my mind, an unanswered plea for understanding.

In the quiet shadows, I observed Aaditi and Vedh, their connection flowing effortlessly, like a secret language that excluded me from its comprehension. Each shared moment, every exchanged glance, cut through me like a knife, a silent betrayal etched in the fabric of their shared happiness.

The choices that led Aaditi away from my orbit became haunting questions, a desperate pursuit to decipher the mystery of her heart. The unraveling scene before me was a painful spectacle, a front-row seat to the fading echoes of my deepest desires.

As a silent witness to Aaditi's newfound joy, the ache within me deepened. The pain of watching her slip away once again carved scars into my soul, whispering tales of unspoken longing and the bitter residue of unrequited love.

In the shadows of my contemplation, a plan emerged—a deliberate move to disrupt Aaditi and Vedh's seemingly unbreakable bond. The fear of losing her intensified my resolve, propelling me to rewrite the script of their relationship.

With calculated steps, I aimed to unravel the threads that tied Aaditi and Vedh together. The desperation to be the source of her happiness fueled my determination.

In this pursuit, there was no room for acceptance of a reality where Aaditi slipped away. The fragility of hope now rested on the belief that, through deliberate actions, I could rewrite her story—a story where her happiness hinged solely on me.

After a while of Naina keeping a low profile, we finally caught up. Her gaze was questioning, curiosity dancing in her eyes. "What's going on, Rudy? You seem so intense," she remarked.

Taking a deep breath, I leaned in, ready to unravel a narrative that would change the course of Aaditi and Vedh's relationship. "Naina, I've seen things, heard things. Vedh is not who Aaditi thinks he is. He's a threat to her well-being, and we need to protect her."

Naina's brows furrowed in concern, a natural response to my unexpected revelation. "What do you mean, Rudhay? Vedh seems like a nice guy."

I met her gaze with intensity, choosing my words carefully. "Trust me, Naina. Beneath that nice exterior lies a different truth. We can't let Aaditi be blinded by his charm. We need to open her eyes before it's too late."

As I laid out the plan, painting Vedh as a potential danger to Aaditi, I saw a shift in Naina's expression. Skepticism transformed into understanding, and I seized the opportunity to play on her emotions. I appealed to her loyalty and tapped into her grievances with Aarav, convincing her that our actions were justified for Aaditi's well-being.

"Rudhay, this is risky. Are you sure about this?" Naina asked a hint of hesitation in her voice.

Locking eyes with her, I conveyed my determination. "Naina, we can't let Aaditi slip away. We have to do whatever it takes to protect her. Are you with me?"

Naina nodded, a fire of determination igniting in her eyes. "I'm with you, Rudhay. Let's make sure she gets the happiness she deserves."

Our alliance was sealed, and our plan was set in motion. Naina, now a willing partner in crime, embraced her role with fervor. Our conversations became strategic discussions, plotting orchestrated encounters, planting seeds of doubt, and carefully cultivating our newfound alliance with Aaditi.

As we delved deeper into the intricate web of Aaditi and Vedh's relationship, the lines between truth and deception blurred. The pieces of our plot fell into place with finesse, orchestrated chaos that seemed to be working. Little did we realize the far-reaching consequences of the web of deceit we had woven—a story that would leave scars not only on Vedh but also on those entangled in our plot.

Throughout the process, a single thought echoed in my mind, a mantra that fueled my determination: "Aaditi deserves only me."

Feeling the pressure closing in, a malicious smile crept across my face as I plotted a scheme to manipulate the situation to my advantage. I planned to break things between Aaditi and Vedh by using Aarav.

"If I can plant doubt between Vedh and Aaditi, they'll be too busy sorting out their own issues to interfere with my plans."

With a twisted satisfaction, I began fabricating a series of fake conversations, carefully molding a narrative designed to cast doubt on Aarav's intentions and create discord between

Vedh and Aaditi. The messages hinted at Aarav's alleged involvement in the entire situation, painting a picture that would leave Aaditi questioning her trust in Vedh.

As I reveled in the deceit, I sent the fabricated messages to Aarav, strategically timing their delivery to coincide with the critical moments of the rescue mission. I anticipated that Aarav, desperate to clear his name and regain Aaditi's trust, would inevitably show her the damning conversations.

In my twisted mind, this calculated move was a means to further manipulate the unfolding events. By sowing the seeds of doubt, I aimed to distract Aarav and Vedh, allowing me to maintain control over the situation and pursue Aaditi without interference.

As the fake messages reached Aarav's phone, I eagerly awaited the chaos I hoped would ensue, confident that this deceitful ploy would create the perfect diversion to advance my dark agenda.

Chapter 12

Wicked Gambit Unleashed

The room, buzzing with tension, suddenly fell silent as the doorbell rang unexpectedly. Confusion washed over us; the gang exchanged uncertain glances, each member wondering who could be at the door at such a crucial time.

As I approached the door, Vedh, Aarav, and Naina stood ready, a mix of apprehension and resolve etched across their faces. The unexpected arrival threw a wrench into our carefully laid plans, and the air crackled with uncertainty.

Upon opening the door, shock and disbelief painted our expressions. Standing there, an unsettling smirk playing on his face, was Rudhay—the very puppet master we had been strategizing to expose.

Rudhay: "Surprised to see me?"

His tone dripped with arrogance, and a predatory glint sparkled in his eyes. The room, once a fortress of determination, now felt like a vulnerable battleground where the tables had turned unexpectedly.

His jaw clenched, and he managed to speak through the tension as Vedh said, "What are you doing here?"

Rudhay's smirk widened, savoring the moment. "I heard you were planning a little intervention. Thought I'd drop by and see what all the fuss is about."

Aarav, his fists involuntarily tightening, shot back, "You won't get away with this. We know everything."

He let out a sinister chuckle, the sound sending shivers down our spines as it reverberated in the dimly lit room. His gaze locked onto us, and with a sly smile, he spoke, "Do you? Well then, let's hear it."

I couldn't help but fire back, "What do you want, Rudhay? You can't just barge in here."

Unfazed, he smirked, taking a leisurely step into the room, "Oh, but I can. This is as much my playground as it is yours."

Attempting to maintain composure, Vedh jumped in, frustration evident in his voice, "Cut the games, Rudhay. We know about your manipulations, and we won't let you ruin our lives any longer."

Feigning innocence, Rudhay's eyes danced with mischief, "Manipulations? I'm hurt, really. I thought we were friends."

Aarav, his patience wearing thin, retorted, "Friends don't play mind games and manipulate each other, Rudhay."

Unfazed, Rudhay glanced around the room, his gaze lingering on Naina, and he slyly remarked, "Naina, my dear, didn't you have something to tell them? Or were you planning on keeping our little secret?"

Naina, visibly rattled, sought support from the gang with a desperate glance. Little did she know that Rudhay had hidden a camera and microphone in her clutch, capturing every moment of her distress.

"I... I don't know what he's talking about," she stammered.

Vedh, sensing Rudhay's manipulative tactics, intervened, "Enough, Rudhay. We're not here to entertain your games. What are you really after?"

Rudhay's mask of feigned innocence cracked, revealing a glint of malice beneath, "Fine, you want the truth? I'm here to expose your little plan. I know everything."

The gang exchanged wary glances, uncertainty flickering in their eyes. Rudhay's unexpected revelation and the violation of Naina's privacy added a layer of complexity to the already volatile situation.

I couldn't hold back any longer, demanding answers, "What are you talking about, Rudhay? What do you think you know?"

Reveling in the discomfort he had sown, Rudhay circled around the room with a predatory swagger, "Oh, I've been watching your little scheme unfold. Planning to expose me, were you? Well, I beat you to the punch."

Aarav, his frustration bubbling to the surface, took a bold step forward. "Enough of your delusional rants, Rudhay. What's your real agenda here?"

A sinister glint danced in Rudhay's narrowed eyes. "I know about your gang, your little plan to expose me. But guess what? I've got evidence, too."

Naina, anxiety painting her features, shot a desperate glance at the gang. The revelation had thrown their carefully laid plans into disarray.

Naina: "What evidence? What's he talking about?"

With a chilling calmness, Rudhay pulled a smartphone from his pocket, reveling in the chaos he'd unleashed.

Rudhay: "I've recorded every conversation, every move. You can't outsmart me."

Unease settled over the gang as they exchanged uncertain glances. Rudhay's calculated moves had shifted the dynamics, leaving them on shaky ground.

Vedh, attempting to maintain composure, spoke up. "Even if you have recordings, it won't change the truth. We won't let you keep manipulating us."

He had a sinister grin persisting, his confidence unshaken. "We'll see about that. The night is young, and the game has just begun."

I couldn't hold back, my frustration boiling over. "Playing mind games won't alter reality, Rudhay. Your manipulations won't endure."

Rudhay's mocking voice cut through the tense atmosphere, "Truth? You're all so naive. The truth is whatever I want it to be."

Aarav, a mix of anger and determination etched on his face, couldn't take any more.

"Enough of this nonsense. Why are you here? What's your endgame?"

Still tightly clutching the phone like a weapon, Rudhay smirked, unveiling a new layer to his sinister plan.

Him: "I'm here with an offer, a chance to spare the rest of you from the storm I'm about to unleash. It's a simple proposition."

The room fell silent, everyone on edge, waiting to hear the unsettling terms Rudhay was about to lay out.

Vedh, breaking the heavy silence, cautiously inquired, "What kind of deal are you proposing?"

Rudhay, relishing the attention, revealed his condition with an unsettling grin. "Hand over Aaditi to me, and I'll provide you with a clean slate. You all walk away, and I get to revel in the chaos as your lives crumble without my interference. She's the key to your salvation—or destruction, depending on your perspective."

Sarah, Monish, Vedh, Aarav, and I exchanged wary glances. The weight of Rudhay's proposal hung heavy in the room, tempting yet treacherous.

Me: "And if we refuse?"

His grin widened, the glint in his eyes intensifying. "Well, then I release everything. Your secrets, your plans, the works. Let's see how well your friendships withstand the fallout."

As the tension thickened, Rudhay added a dark twist to his proposition.

Rudhay: "Oh, and by the way, I have Aaditi's sex tape along with Vedh. I saw you two making out in a parking lot. You guys could have got a room. I can spread it wide, revealing secrets in my hands that can ruin each of your lives. The choice is yours—comply and protect your little secrets, or resist and watch your world crumble."

Rudhay's unsettling proposal was a toxic cloud of manipulation and deceit. With the weight of his ultimatum, they exchanged tense glances. It became clear that Rudhay's obsession with me was not merely a twisted game; it was the linchpin of his sinister plan.

Vedh, his jaw clenched, confronted Rudhay with a mix of anger and disbelief.

"You're using Aaditi as leverage? What do you want from her?"

Rudhay's smirk widened, and the darkness in his intentions laid bare.

Rudhay: "Oh, Vedh, my dear friend, Aaditi is the key to your undoing. I want her."

A chilling silence settled over the room as the weight of Rudhay's words sank in. The gang, realizing the depth of his obsession, braced themselves for the sinister revelation that followed.

Rudhay: "I've always wanted Aaditi. If she agrees to be with me willingly, I'll hand over all the evidence. But if she refuses, well, your secrets become public knowledge."

Aarav's anger flared, unable to contain his disgust at Rudhay's depraved proposition.

"You think Aaditi will ever choose you over Vedh? You're delusional."

Rudhay scoffed, a sinister smile playing on his lips. "Aarav, you don't understand. Aaditi will choose me because she has to. It's not about deserving; it's about destiny. She's always belonged to me, and she always will. Neither you nor Vedh can compare to the connection we share."

With a self-assured tone, Rudhay continued, "You guys don't know the vulnerable side of Aaditi when she was all alone. I was her pillar, the one who understood her in ways you can't comprehend. I've wanted to marry her since childhood. Do you even know her likes and dislikes? I know every bit of her, even the things she doesn't realize about herself. Our connection goes beyond surface-level understanding; it's a deep, intrinsic bond that you and Vedh can never replicate."

Rudhay's conviction echoed through the room as he proclaimed, "Aaditi is mine, and she will always choose me, now and forever. Our connection is unbreakable, and no one, not even Vedh or you, can stand in the way of our destiny."

"No, Rudhay, you are wrong. What I had for Aarav were true feelings, genuine emotions that you can't just break apart. And now, with Vedh, he is the love of my life. You can't force someone to be with you, to feel something they don't. Love is a natural, beautiful connection built on affection, trust, and understanding. It can't be coerced or manipulated.

You may claim to know every bit of me, but love isn't about possession; it's about mutual respect and shared happiness. I won't be swayed by your misguided notions of destiny. I have the right to choose who I want in my life, and it's not something that can be dictated by anyone else.

Aarav and Vedh have both shown me what true companionship is, and I won't let you undermine the genuine connections I've formed. Love is a choice, and my heart belongs to the one who respects and cherishes it, not someone who tries to impose their will upon it."

Caught in a twisted game where the stakes were not just our secrets but the well-being of Aaditi. The realization that Rudhay's obsession had reached such dangerous heights fueled a collective determination to protect Aaditi from his shitty game.

He, unmoved by their protests, maintained his cold composure. "We will see that. Now the clock is ticking. Aaditi has a choice to make. Think wisely, my friends."

Aarav: "You're not taking Aaditi anywhere, Rudhay!"

Rudhay, reveling in the chaos he had sown, chuckled darkly." Love makes people do crazy things, Aarav. We'll see just how crazy Aaditi is willing to get."

Aarav lunged forward, attempting to block Rudhay's path. However, Rudhay, unfazed, revealed a chilling secret—a gun tucked in his waistband.

Rudhay: "Back off, Aarav. I have no qualms about using this."

The glint of the weapon sent a shiver through the room, paralyzed by the sudden escalation, grappling with the reality that their pursuit of justice had taken a perilous turn.

I was caught in the middle of the power struggle and pleaded with Rudhay.

"Rudhay, please, this isn't the way. Let us go, and we'll figure this out without anyone getting hurt."

His grip on me tightened, and he sneered at Aarav.

Rudhay: "Aarav, you've always underestimated me. Now, step aside or face the consequences."

Torn between the fear for my safety and the threat of Rudhay's firearm, Aarav reluctantly took a step back. The room once filled with determination, now resonated with the haunting reality that Rudhay was willing to resort to violence to achieve his twisted desires.

Seizing the opportunity, Rudhay maneuvered me toward the door, leaving the gang paralyzed in his wake. The chilling sound of the door slamming shut echoed in the room, marking Rudhay's escape with me in tow.

As the gang grappled with the shock of the unfolding events, a heavy silence descended. The weight of their choices and the imminent threat posed by Rudhay's escape lingered. The night, which had started with a mission to expose the manipulator, now veered into uncharted territory—a dark and uncertain path where the consequences of our decisions had become a haunting reality.

Aarav, his frustration evident, lashed out, "What the hell, Aaditi? How could you go with Rudhay? Don't you care about yourself? Do you even realize the danger you're putting yourself in?"

Vedh, equally enraged, added, "This is insane! Rudhay is dangerous, and you can't just throw yourself into the lion's den like this. Do you have any idea what he's capable of?"

As the reality sank in, panic replaced their initial anger. Both Aarav and Vedh realized the gravity of the situation and the urgency to locate me before any harm could befall me. They frantically grabbed their phones, desperately attempting to contact me.

While Aarav and Vedh raced against time to find me, Sarah, displaying unwavering concern, decided to take a proactive approach. She reached out to my dad, her voice tinged with urgency and determination.

Sarah: "Uncle, it's Sarah. There's a serious problem. Aaditi is in danger. Rudhay has taken her, and Aarav and Vedh are on their way to rescue her."

My dad's concerned silence echoed through the phone before he responded with palpable worry: "What? Where are they? What's happening?"

He could almost feel the tension in Sarah's voice as she quickly briefed him on the unfolding situation, sharing details about Rudhay's involvement and emphasizing the urgency of the rescue mission. Understanding the gravity of the issue, my dad assured Sarah that he would take immediate action.

Dad: "Thank you for letting me know, Sarah. I'm on my way. I'll contact the authorities right away. We need to ensure Aaditi's safety. Meantime, keep me updated on their location."

As Sarah hung up, a sense of relief washed over me, knowing that my dad was stepping in and involving the authorities to aid in the search for Rudhay and me. The unfolding drama had now extended its reach, bringing the force of law into play to put an end to Rudhay's dangerous actions.

Aarav, pacing with frustration, exclaimed, "We need to find her location. She can't be far. I can't believe she would willingly go with Rudhay."

Vedh, typing rapidly on his phone, replied, "I shared my location with her. Let me check where she is." As he scanned the map, his expression shifted from anger to deep concern. "Damn it, her location is not updating. Something's wrong."

Meanwhile, Rudhay and I drove near a hidden retreat—an old mansion that, oddly enough, was a gift from my dad to Rudhay's family. The weight of secrets made the atmosphere mysterious and unsettling.

Trapped in the clutches of Rudhay's dark obsession, I desperately attempted to reason with him.

I pleaded, "Rudhay, you can't force someone to love you. Let me go, and we can find a way to resolve this."

Rudhay, his obsession reaching unsettling heights, responded with a maniacal gleam in his eyes. Suddenly, he closed the distance between us, attempting to kiss me. Instinctively, I stepped back, my anger simmering beneath the surface.

My frustration burst forth, and I told him with a forceful intensity, "Be a man, Rudhay! Stop playing these games. Stop toying with me." The words hung heavy, a defiant challenge in the face of his twisted desires.

Undeterred, Rudhay sneered, "You have no idea how many years I've been craving to have you in my arms. You belong to me." His possessive declaration sent a shiver down my spine, intensifying the dark and dangerous atmosphere that surrounded us.

Aarav: "Damn it, Vedh! Why would Aaditi go with Rudhay willingly? This makes no sense!"

Vedh, his face etched with concern, replied while keeping an eye on the updating location: "I don't know, Aarav. We need to find her first. We'll deal with the 'why' later."

Aarav, clenching his jaw, muttered: "She can be impulsive, but this is a whole new level. Rudhay is dangerous, and she's willingly putting herself in harm's way."

Vedh, glancing at Aarav, added: "We need to focus on getting her out of there safely. We can figure out the rest later."

As they turned a corner, the location updated, indicating they were getting closer. The tension in the air was palpable as they quickened their pace, anxiety hanging heavy between them.

Aarav, his voice filled with urgency: "Vedh, we're running out of time. We have to make sure she's okay."

Vedh nodded in agreement, his determination matching Aarav's: "We're almost there. Let's get Aaditi out of this mess.

The duo sped through the city streets, guided solely by the last known location. With each passing moment, the worry intensified, fueled by the uncertainty of what might be happening to me. The streets became a labyrinth, and Vedh's heart raced as they closed in on the location.

Finally arriving at the destination, they were met with an eerie silence. The old mansion stood before them, cloaked in shadows. Vedh, fueled by concern and determination, kicked open the door, revealing a scene of unsettling tension.

Rudhay, caught off guard by the sudden intrusion, struggled against Aarav's hold. Aaditi, visibly distressed, pleaded for an end to the ordeal. Vedh, fueled by relief and anger, stepped forward, his gaze fixed on Rudhay.

The situation hung in the balance as Vedh demanded, "Let her go, Rudhay! This ends now." The room, once filled with darkness and uncertainty, now teetered on the edge of resolution, awaiting the outcome of Vedh's plea.

With a dangerous glint in his eyes, Rudhay declared, "You guys won't let me be with Aaditi? Then I'll make sure she won't be with anyone – not with you, not with Vedh, not with anyone!"

Desperation fueled my attempt to reason with him, "Rudhay, please, let me go. We can find a way to resolve this without anyone getting hurt." The room held its breath, waiting for the volatile situation to unfold, trapped in a narrative of uncertainty and danger.

Aarav, catching Vedh's signal, feigned a momentary distraction, allowing Vedh to discreetly activate a recording feature on his phone. Unbeknownst to Rudhay, the device silently captured the escalating confrontation, preserving evidence of his threats and menacing behavior.

As Rudhay continued his ominous declarations, Vedh strategically maneuvered to ensure the phone's inconspicuous recording kept capturing the unfolding events. Aarav, keeping Rudhay engaged in conversation, played along with the ruse, buying time for the critical evidence to be collected.

Aarav: "Rudhay, listen, there has to be another way. We don't want anyone getting hurt here. Just let Aaditi go, and we can talk about this."

Rudhay, still gripped by his delusions, hesitated for a moment, considering Aarav's words. Little did he know that his threats were being meticulously recorded, creating a crucial piece of evidence that could be used against him.

Vedh, having successfully secured the incriminating recording, discreetly sent the file to Sarah, who had been coordinating with my dad and the authorities. Unaware of the turn of events, Rudhay continued to monologue about his possessive desires.

In a sudden turn of events, the door burst open as the authorities, armed and ready, stormed into the room. The sudden intrusion caught Rudhay off guard, and his grip on me momentarily loosened. Aarav seized the opportunity, pulling me away from Rudhay's grasp.

Authority Figure: "Rudhay Malik, you are under arrest for kidnapping and making threats. Put the weapon down!"

Rudhay, realizing the tables had turned against him, glared at Aarav and Vedh, his eyes filled with rage and frustration.

Rudhay: "You think this changes anything? She will always be mine! I'll never let Aaditi be with you, Vedh!"

Before anyone could react, Aarav, displaying a selfless instinct, lunged in between Vedh and the impending danger. The deafening sound of gunfire echoed through the room, and in a fraction of a second, the air became thick with tension as Aarav, with a pained expression, crumpled to the ground.

Vedh, his eyes widening in shock, reached out to Aarav, his hands stained with disbelief and horror. The room fell into a haunting silence, Aarav, gasping for breath, clutched his chest, blood staining his fingers. Vedh, paralyzed by shock, knelt beside his friend, desperate to staunch the bleeding.

As the authorities swiftly apprehended Rudhay, the room transitioned from chaos to a grim aftermath. Vedh, grappling with shock, turned his attention to Aarav, who lay on the floor, his pallor growing paler with each passing moment.

Vedh: "Aarav, hang in there! Help is on the way."

Despite Vedh's attempts to reassure him, Aarav's focus remained unwaveringly on Aaditi's well-being. He continued to murmur, "Take care of Aaditi," his voice strained yet resolute.

Vedh, torn between attending to Aarav and the impending arrival of the ambulance, took a moment to reach out to Sarah, who had been coordinating with the authorities.

Vedh: "Sarah, Aarav got shot. We need an ambulance urgently."

Sarah, her voice steady yet filled with concern, assured Vedh that help was on the way. As the distant wail of sirens grew nearer, Vedh and I did our best to make Aarav as comfortable as possible while waiting for professional medical assistance.

When the ambulance finally arrived, the paramedics took charge, working swiftly to stabilize Aarav's condition. Vedh and I, gripped by the weight of the recent events, followed the ambulance to the hospital, where Aarav would undergo urgent medical care.

In the hospital waiting room, time seemed to stretch endlessly as we anxiously awaited news about Aarav's condition. The sterile white walls echoed the hushed murmurs of worried conversations around us, creating an atmosphere of tense anticipation.

Vedh and I, both emotionally drained, exchanged glances that spoke volumes about the shared concern for our friend and the complexity of the events that had unfolded. The gravity of Aarav's sacrifice hung heavily in the air, and the lingering echoes of Rudhay's dark obsession intensified the somber mood.

After what felt like an eternity, a weary-looking doctor approached us. Vedh and I rose in unison, anticipation etched on our faces.

Despite the initial positive signs, a sudden turn of events cast a shadow over our fragile sense of relief. Aarav, while seemingly on the path to recovery, unexpectedly slipped into a coma.

The news struck us like a sudden storm, leaving Vedh and me grappling with a renewed wave of worry and uncertainty. The hospital room, once a place of tentative recovery, transformed into a somber space where the beeping of medical monitors now sounded more ominous than before.

Vedh and I spent hours by Aarav's bedside, navigating the complex emotions that accompanied this unforeseen development.

The hospital atmosphere became charged with tension as my dad arrived, worry etched across his face. His eyes darted around the room, searching for me, and when he spotted Vedh and me, the lines on his forehead deepened with concern.

Dad: "What the hell happened? Why is my daughter in the middle of all this chaos?"

I could feel the intensity of his protective instincts and the need to explain the complex events leading up to Aarav's injury, and my safety weighed heavily on Vedh and me.

Without hesitation, I rushed into my dad's arms, seeking solace. Tears streamed down my face as I confessed, "It's all my fault, Dad. Because of me, Aarav is now in a coma."

Vedh, gathering himself, took a deep breath and began recounting the harrowing events of that fateful night – the tense confrontation with Rudhay, Aarav's selfless act, and the subsequent developments that led to Aarav slipping into a coma. My dad's anger simmered beneath the surface as he absorbed the gravity of the situation, creating an emotionally charged tableau in that somber hospital room.

Amidst the quiet hum of medical equipment, the door creaked open, revealing a somber-faced police officer. He exchanged a few words with the medical staff before turning to us.

Officer: "We need your cooperation for a statement regarding the events that unfolded."

As we began to recount the night's chaos, the officer's stern expression hinted at the gravity of the situation. Little did we know that Rudhay, in a desperate attempt to escape authorities, had not gone far.

Outside the hospital, the night air was charged with tension. Rudhay, fueled by a mix of fear and aggression, had managed to evade initial attempts at capture. The authorities, however, were closing in.

In a dramatic turn, Rudhay cornered and with nowhere to run, brandishing a weapon. The hospital entrance transformed into a scene of heightened danger as the authorities, forced to defend themselves and protect those in the vicinity, fired at Rudhay.

The echoing shots reverberated through the night, a cacophony of chaos that reached the hospital corridors. Vedh and I, still reeling from the earlier events, were shielded from the immediate danger but were acutely aware of the unfolding crisis.

The authorities, acting swiftly to neutralize the threat, aimed for Rudhay's leg in an attempt to incapacitate rather than cause fatal harm. The tense standoff reached its climax as Rudhay crumpled to the ground, writhing in pain.

The hospital's emergency response team, alerted by the sudden commotion, rushed to the scene. The once-quiet hospital entrance was now a battleground between law enforcement and a man consumed by a dark obsession.

Rudhay, injured and unable to escape, was swiftly apprehended by the authorities. The gravity of the situation sank in as the hospital staff ushered us away from the unfolding drama.

As Rudhay was led away in custody, the authorities ensured that he received medical attention for his leg wound, and a surreal sense of closure settled over the chaotic night. The hospital entrance, once a place of healing, had witnessed a tumultuous climax to a series of events that had forever changed the course of our lives.

Two years had passed since that tumultuous night that altered the course of our lives. The echoes of the events still lingered, but time had begun to heal some of the wounds. Vedh and I navigated the aftermath of Aarav's sacrifice, finding solace in the enduring bonds that had withstood the trials of that fateful night.

The legal proceedings had taken their course, and Rudhay declared mentally unstable, found himself confined to a remand home for the mentally unstable. Although I visited him once, his words echoed hauntingly in my mind – "I knew you'd come. Love, you will always come for me." Yet, my visit wasn't fueled by compassion for Rudhay but by the need to confront the news that had reached us.

Aarav, the selfless hero of that chaotic night, had passed away. The news struck us with the force of a relentless storm, leaving us grappling with grief and the harsh reality of his absence. The hospital room, where we had hoped for recovery, now held the weight of memories and unfulfilled dreams.

As I stood outside the remand home, the cold wind carrying the whispers of the past, I couldn't help but reflect on the journey we had undertaken. The scars of that night, both visible and hidden, were a testament to the resilience of the human spirit.

The legal system had deemed Rudhay unfit for society, a consequence of the darkness that had consumed him. Aarav's sacrifice, Vedh's steadfast friendship, and my own resilience had become intertwined threads in the tapestry of our collective story.

The remand home, with its barred windows and somber atmosphere, stood as a stark reminder of the choices made and the paths taken. As I turned away, the weight of the past gradually lifted, replaced by a bittersweet acknowledgment that life, though marked by loss and struggle, continued to unfold.

The road ahead was uncertain, but the enduring strength of friendship and the lessons learned from the trials of that night would guide us forward. The echoes of Aarav's courage, Vedh's loyalty, and the resolution of a chaotic chapter resonated in our hearts, shaping the narrative of our lives as we ventured into an uncertain future.

As I moved forward, determined to rebuild my life, Rudhay's mind took a different turn within the confines of the remand home. In his room, he found solace in his art. The once-disturbed individual appeared to be finding a strange sense of happiness as he took to sketching.

One day, Rudhay found himself inspired to draw a portrait of me. The strokes on paper captured a version of me that he had once obsessed over. Surprisingly, his demeanor transformed as he immersed himself in the creative process. Laughter echoed within the walls of his room as he worked on his artistic endeavor.

Upon completing the portrait, Rudhay affixed it to his wall with a sense of accomplishment. As he gazed at the drawing, a twisted satisfaction flickered in his eyes. With a chilling determination, he jotted down a single phrase in a small notebook he kept: "One down, one more to go."

Unbeknownst to him, his misguided notion of possession and control over me was just a fading shadow in the face of the resilience and strength that had emerged from the trials of that fateful night. While Rudhay remained trapped in his delusions, Vedh and I continued to carve out a future that honored the memory of our lost friend, Aarav.

The world outside moved forward, leaving Rudhay in the past, and as I focused on healing and rebuilding, the echoes of his disturbing thoughts became nothing more than whispers in the wind.